MW00897806

THE 4TH
WATCH

The Assignment

RS NEWMAN

ISBN 978-1-64458-544-3 (paperback)
ISBN 978-1-64492-087-9 (hardcover)
ISBN 978-1-64458-545-0 (digital)

Copyright © 2019 by RS Newman

All rights reserved. No part of this publication may be reproduced, distributed, or transmitted in any form or by any means, including photocopying, recording, or other electronic or mechanical methods without the prior written permission of the publisher. For permission requests, solicit the publisher via the address below.

Christian Faith Publishing, Inc.
832 Park Avenue
Meadville, PA 16335
www.christianfaithpublishing.com

Printed in the United States of America

Chapter 1

"Which one's yours?"

"That one right there, the dirty blonde with freckles jumping off that slide. Her name's Emily."

"She's cute."

"Thanks, how about you? Which one's yours?"

"Mine is that little one right there, in the pink outfit with brown hair and blue eyes following your Emily. That's my Sara, my love."

They both stare in amazement at the purity of two three-year-old girls, as their imaginations are let loose while at the local park. Standing at just the right distance to give the young ones their space to play, but close enough to jump in there if an incident were to occur.

"Is she your first?"

"Emily? Oh yeah. It's changing me. I see this whole life thing in such a new light. It's so beyond what I thought it was. It's just so precious and fragile, you know what I mean?" Ramiel asks as he cautiously lets out a heavy sigh, not wanting to disturb the atmosphere.

"Yeah, I get it. This whole process has been an eye-opener for me, too. I didn't know I could love like this before Sara came into my life. Everything before this was just work, work, work. And work is good, I'm thankful for it, and what it is. But this, this has changed me. Sara's opened my eyes." Sariel fixes his eyes on Sara as he finishes his sentence and gazes as if his sight were a shield of protection for her.

"So, I take it she's your first, too?" Ramiel asks, breaking Sariel's attention.

"Yes sir, first ever." He grins as he continues to watch the girls play.

"How rude of me, I'm Ramiel." He motions to shake his hand.

"Oh yeah, sorry, I'm Sariel." They shake hands and complete their introductions.

"So how long have you been here, Ramiel?"

Crash. The conversation is quickly interrupted as a sound of hard contact is made behind the two beings talking. They both look over their shoulders to see three figures standing and conversing as they sheath their weapons after dealing with a would-be intruder. No alarms are raised, so they return to their conversation.

"That was loud. Anyway, we've been here since Emily's birth. You?"

"We just moved to the area a few days ago from DC. This is our first day out and about, but from what I've seen so far, I'm happy to be away from the city."

"Oh yeah, why's that?"

"This suburban life looks like a nice break from where we came." Sariel takes in a quick look at his surroundings and then returns his gaze to Sara.

"Yeah, well it's not all peachy here, today's just been a quiet day so far. There are plenty of struggles and confrontations here in the suburbs, my friend. However, coming from DC, I can imagine this feels like a nice break for you."

For Sariel, the lack of people is a welcome break compared to the millions in DC. Downtown buildings and skyscrapers are replaced with two-story homes and shopping centers. Mobs getting on the subway are replaced with moms looking for the closest parking spot at the local food market. The neighborhood itself is outlined with a massive eight-foot brick wall but open entryways. Houses are stacked on each other with very little breathing room, as if they were seats in a commercial airliner. The park is centrally located to the rectangular layout of the subdivision, containing slides, swings, monkey bars, walls to climb, a sandbox to play in, and more. It's the oasis for this barren desert of homes that resemble sand dunes that go on and on and on.

"What did you do before you got here? Not here, as in the suburbs, but before this new gig entirely. What was your background in?" Ramiel asks as he motions his hand behind him, as if pointing at the past.

"Before this? Well, before this I was in accounting. I took record of every action that was set before me. During the busy times, I could have five or six accounts, but typically I averaged three. I marked choices, actions, verbiage, body language, reactions, thoughts, and just about everything else. I thought it might help with this new job, but it really hasn't.

"It's different now because I wasn't emotionally involved like I am now, you know? Now it's personal, I feel like I have a vested interest in this job. At least I like to think I do, anyway's. How about you, what did you do before this?"

"I was in communications. Primarily, weather patterns. I would transfer coordinates for certain events and relay messages from home to certain weather elements here to make sure they complied. It was cool to be able to see and form a hurricane over the ocean, or watch the earth transform as it grew from volcanic expansion. Sometimes, I would be allowed to do the really entertaining stuff, and I would be able to message with the galaxy and its stars. Regardless, I really didn't have any interaction with humanity before this, so this was all brand new to me."

"So how was that transfer? Did you struggle any at first? Is it everything you thought it would be?" Sariel breaks eye contact from Sara to hear, to intently focus on Ramiel's answer, as if his body language would give Sariel the truth he was searching for.

"You mean being a protector? I absolutely love it. It's what I had hoped for but also so much more. I don't believe I will ever forget that day that it became official. When He told me about Emily and how much He loves her and how I'm supposed to watch over her, it hit me hard. Like a shooting star bursting through a black hole, not knowing where its final destination would end.

"I didn't know then what I know now, but I'm still glad I got to take the assignment." Ramiel reaches out to stroke Emily's hair, as if her touch is the anchor that keeps him stationed here and not back home.

"That was really beautiful. I feel the same way about Sara. While He was telling me all about her, I didn't know if I could love her so intensely, but once I got here and saw her in that delivery room, something in me just changed. Almost as if I could see her through His eyes. It's been a battle from day one, but she's worth the fight." Sariel then canvasses the playground, taking in his surroundings as his statement reminds him of his purpose. Sariel begins to relax as their conversation continues, and he gets more acquainted with his surroundings and new friend.

Their job is a battle, and both Sariel and Ramiel are here to fight it. As Sariel scans the area, his head turns as a lighthouse beacon would, pointing out treachery that awaits the unknowing and unseeing travelers. There are fourteen children ranging in age from three to eight currently at the park. Each child with its own protector standing nearby, ready for what could come. Each protector varies in size, but they all are giants when compared to man. Their angel wings line their back like tight jackets on a cold day. They don't get in the way, but when they are being used, they spread like the majesty of an eagle in flight. Each hip is adorned with a sword, one for each hand, allowing the most amount of damage possible. Currently, to the naked eye, these protectors would look as if they were wearing robes like in Roman times, until an altercation would arise and activate their armor. As Sara and Emily get older and interact more with the world, Sariel and Ramiel find themselves activating their armor more often.

Also, in the proximity are knowers and two followers. Knowers are people that have come to a point in life to choose for themselves whether to believe or not. A couple of them have made a choice to believe and to follow; hence, the title of follower. They have chosen more than just the idea of Him, but have chosen Him. They are accompanied by their original protector who has, in return for their choice, been upgraded. As well as three additional warrior angels, all of them have taken positions around their knower. One for the north, south, east, and west. The upgraded protector always has his armor on and typically has grown in size by at least one foot. This growth comes from the maturity of their follower. The more the follower believes and the deeper the relationship goes, the bigger the protector gets. This also happens because the protector typically fights off the enemy more often and fights a harsher barrage from the legions of the fallen. They are on the front lines of the spiritual battlefield, and their size and presence need to represent strength and victory.

Outside of the playground equipment, children, protectors, followers, and knowers, there are thousands upon thousands of these fallen—also known as demons. They were given the name "fallen" by the angels that didn't fall in the great war. They believed the great deceiver's lie, and now they spread it like cancer to any frail host, destroying anything in their path. These creatures of darkness don't compare in size anymore to their old brothers of light because of their choice. They are weaker now and are no longer protected by life. They reek of death and struggle to hold themselves up. They have a toxic mist about them that infects knowers if they hang around them too long. They are skinny, like a malnourished corpse that has recently been found and rescued from swampy waters. The only two advantages they have, if you want to call it that, are the knower's gift of choice and the ability to use them as portals from their realm to this one.

Knowers can be weak and will choose more often for the instant gratification rather than the long race of eternity. These fallen take advantage of that and fill them with lies and deceit about days of tomorrow and for them to live in the now. The protectors are there to stop as much as possible; but typically, they find themselves struggling against the fallen and their host parents. It takes most, if not all, of the protector's strength to keep the fallen off and away from their little ones. They aren't able to clean house for knowers and do their job effectively, so the little ones are the priority always.

However, this park at this particular time is currently a safe haven for these children. The strength of the angels are too much for the fallen to pick an easy fight. They know the night is coming, and the group will eventually disperse to their individual homes. So they cowardly wait on the outskirts of the park, like hyenas waiting to pick off the weak and devour them one by one.

"This is nice here so far. I see we have company around us, but not like DC. There were some big ones there. I even saw two dragons one time." Sariel states as he brings his gaze back to Sara.

"Really, two dragons? That must have been a sight. I've been lucky not to have seen any of those here yet, but you never know. I wonder which two fallen arches those were. Did you get a close enough look?" Ramiel cautiously asks as he puts both hands on his weapons to prepare, as if the dragons would arrive any second.

"No, they were a decent distance away, but they definitely stood out. Even though they don't have life anymore, they still are mammoths in size and stature. I would never want to face one alone if I didn't have to." Sariel states as he looks down and through the earth. As if staring straight into the abyss, contemplating how he might even attack a creature of that size.

"I'm with you on that. Until my little Emily makes that choice, I don't think I would be ready for a fight like that either. Well regardless, you're not in DC anymore, and I will help out as often as possible if I am able to, my new friend."

"Thanks, Ramiel, I really appreciate that. I will as well."

Both protectors continue in conversation as time continues to pass. Eventually, the children are called away one at a time by their knowers, and the formidable group of angels and protection begins to dwindle down. Each protector is prepared for this and goes on high alert while they leave the comfort of friends and help. Eventually, Rameil and Sariel are separated as duty pulls them away. They both bid each other farewell until the next time their girls play together.

As Sariel is following Sara and her mom home, he sees more than the usual number of fallen accompanying them tonight. He listens in as Sara's mom, Nancy, grumbles to herself.

"That stupid witch. How did she even come to believe such a lie? Who is spreading this crazy rumor around anyway? We don't even know anyone here. We just moved here, the moving truck isn't even out of the driveway yet. I mean, come on, people. Bill is not going to like this, this is absurd, utterly ridiculous."

The number of fallen has almost doubled around her as the pack of stray dogs gathers for what they think will be an easy meal.

Something apparently was said at the park to set her off like this. In any case, tonight is going to be the first real test for Sariel since moving to the suburbs with Sara. He takes this opportunity while walking home to ready himself for the upcoming battle. He takes out both blades and swings them in circular motions, as if stretching before the night's activities. He scans ahead to check the condition of the home to find that it's already crawling with the enemy.

"Welcome to suburbia, Sariel."

Chapter 2

"Can you believe what they said?" Nancy expels to her husband, Bill, with hands in the air. "They think we moved here because you got demoted or something. They don't bother to ask why we moved. I just had some tramp in the park ask me how we're doing. She went on to ask if you really did lose your job or were demoted. That's what one of the other moms is telling people. How did they even get that idea? We haven't even talked to anyone here. What is going on? That bit—" She continues with her rage with gossip as the kitchen fills beyond capacity with the fallen. They come in through doors, windows, from out of the chests of Bill and Nancy, to then appear to be falling from the ceiling like rain. Her anger and reaction to the malicious gossip presents itself like a buffet to the fallen that fill the room to feed.

Bill is just standing there with his beverage of choice in hand, allowing his wife to vent without any comfort or support—as if he were a trained dog and is assuming his correct position on her command. He is not the leader that he should be, but in fact a doormat that Nancy uses to wipe filth off repeatedly.

"Protector, are you ready to play? We've been working on that line of trash for your female since the moving trucks pulled into the neighborhood." The voice comes from the fallen as if it were a wave of noise trickling over their corpses. Not proceeding from a leader or individual, but instead its sound is presented from the whole as it sweeps through their ranks.

"We're not going to make this easy. We want you to learn properly who is in charge around here. You're solo in this home. No followers, no warriors, no park. Just you. This is going to hurt, and when we're done, your precious little one won't be so pure anymore. In fact,

I think we just may have her ready to make her choice tonight." As the words continue to fly toward Sariel, he notices the fallen wiping tar and death from their mouths as they spew out on every other word and stain the ground upon contact.

"I will grant you one shot at mercy. Leave now and continue your filth of an existence, or stay and learn your end." Sariel strengthens his grip around his blades and assumes a defensive position. His legs bend, and his left foot slides toward the fallen that is closest to him. Both arms rise, one above his head and the other out in front like a shield. The instant they find their final position, the swords ignite with fire, exposing even more the true nature of the fallen. Shriveled skeletons of their once-majestic selves, as if they had abused substances over the course of several lifetimes without fail or break.

"Ha ha," they all laugh together as they pull out their swords and move into attack positions. They surround him like wild dogs, presenting force from every direction, crouching on all surfaces of the home, ready to spring at the first sign of conflict.

"Since we can't kill you, we're just going to hold you down and make you watch." The voice's tone grows deep as it spews its final words. With their arms outstretched and pointed at Sara, they begin to hiss like the serpent they obey. Quickly, all fallen are hissing in unison and the noise grows to a low roar.

"For You have girded me with strength for battle. You have subdued under me those who rose up against me. The Lord is my strength and my shield. My heart trusts in Him, and I am helped. Therefore, my heart exults, and with my song, I shall thank Him," Sariel shouts his war cry as his armor comes into full effect. Glowing white with perfection and craftsmanship, his armor immediately covers him from head to toe. Made with a substance not known to man, the already-formidable and solid-sized angel just transformed into a tower of absolute strength and power. "For the Master. For Sara!"

The battle begins as he finishes her name. To the human eye, it's just a husband and wife bickering and complaining in the kitchen while their daughter sits at the kitchen island eating a quick snack after the park. In the spiritual realm, it's an explosion of smoke and death as the fallen hurl themselves toward the only light source in the vicinity. Man-made objects are not affected by these spiritual beings but in fact are only a canvass for their display.

Ten fallen collapse on Sariel with the swords as he braces for the blow. Four others instantly plunge their cheap metallic blades toward his center. Without hesitation or strain, he parries the ten and jumps and spins in a tornado-like motion, missing the additional four. Before landing on bended knee, he cuts the heads clean off of three of the fallen, and then, as water through a mountainside, he pushes his blades through two others, and then swings his body around as if doing an about-face to separate hips from torsos of six others. The movements are majestic and clean, yet the wave of death and venom continue toward him, not at all affected by his blows.

They press on and forward, trying to consume his current position like a landslide to an unsuspecting road. Through training and experience, he is able to parry the additional attacks. Upon doing so, he buys himself enough time to release his wings and activate his armor. The span of his presence has now grown to over twelve feet in width.

What once appeared as robes and soft clothes now presents itself as metal and fortitude. Immediately, his body is covered from head to toe in a hard metallic substance not known to man. His head is covered completely, except for his eyes and slits over his mouth, allowing his speech to exit more clearly. The armors thickness is more than two inches over his chest and other parts of his body, while in other areas it appears to be slim and covered in a chain-mail-like substance to allow mobility. It's silver in color, but its polish allows the fire from the blades to glisten and distract as it dances off the armor and lands into the eyes of the enemy. The flesh of the feathers and bone are covered by his armor, creating hundreds of tiny blades as they do not waver in the wind.

Now on his feet, both fiery swords in hand and his wings spread like a caution sign to the foolish, he braces for another attack. Ten more fallen collapse on him from above, driving their swords down with all of their strength, and ten additional fallen lunge toward his center to run him through. Again, he parries the blows from on high, but this time his wings form a shield around his midsection, creating a barrier of safety, deflecting the additional blows. After the wings deflect, they turn to their offensive use and begin to move forward and backward, slicing through any spiritual figure in their path. Dozens of fallen drop and vanish to outer darkness, while dozens more take their place and continue the attack.

During the fight, Sara gets up from her seat as she listens to her parents, primarily her mother, continue to complain about their new neighborhood. She makes her way to the fridge as she grabs a premade sippy cup of apple juice before returning to her front-row seat to the show presented before her. While this is happening, Sariel dances around his toddler and keeps any contact whatsoever from reaching its destination on her spiritual being. Raindrops of fire, like sparks from a welding torch, fall around her as blades screech across and down Sariel's swords as he deflects and protects. Before Sara resumes her seat, Sariel launches himself from it and does a backflip through the air, clearing the area of any fallen hoping to get an easy shot at his little one.

This dance of death and light continues for several minutes all around the kitchen as the human inhabitants have no earthly idea as to what is currently raging around them. Finally, the remaining fallen members stop what they are doing and sheath their blades, indicating they are done for now. The voice that once proceeded from their collective begins to speak again.

"Protector, what is your name?" It asks as its tone sounds tired and gasping for air.

"Sariel, son of the Master and follower of His word." He shouts with a triumphant cry, not winded in the slightest, as if his words would incite additional blows.

"Sariel, you're pathetic," the voice says while spitting the words to the ground. "Curse you and die! This is not over, son of the master. This is just the beginning. We will be back. We will have her, and she will be just like her parents. Ungrateful, jealous, weak, and lost. Next time won't be so easy. Until we meet again, protector." The final words hit the floor and dissolve like smoke into the air.

In unison, the horde turns their backs and fly away, leaving behind a stench of death as the corpses of their comrades begin to fade away like dust in the wind. Sariel stands at attention for a few moments before lowering his arms and allowing his helmet to recede and open so he can more clearly observe his surroundings. He watches as Sara is finishing her snack with eyes fixed on her parents. Her mom suddenly changes her tone and states it doesn't matter what others think as long as they have each other. Bill rolls his eyes and braces for his incoming wife. They kiss and move on, all while Sara watches. The lesson was taught, and it was fierce. Cry, complain, cower, and then just move on. Not a single healthy teaching lesson shown to Sara, but rather an example of weakness and gossip.

Sariel sees what has happened and tries to take his small victory best he can. He continues to stand there and is grateful it wasn't worse. As Nancy begins to walk away, a member of the fallen crawls from her mouth and slithers to the floor. Laughing and screeching at Sariel as it exits the room. Three additional fallen leave Bill's chest and arms as if they were holding him down and not allowing him to respond in the way a father and authority figure should have. They also laugh and smirk at Sariel as they exit. Their actions remind the protector again that knowers are gateways for their masters. They can only serve one or the other and are used by their master according to their allegiance. Sariel finally drops his guard and moves toward Sara as she continues to sit. Unbeknownst to Sara, he leans in and kisses the top of her head.

"I love you, and I will protect you until I can't. I'm sorry your parents don't follow, but I pray one day they might, for their sakes and yours."

Sariel then stands straight up again and looks outside. He sees legions of fallen consuming the streets, windows, and the entire block. They are laughing and cackling as they spew death and curses in every direction. Unfortunately, this is an all-too-familiar sight for a protector. They must be on guard at all hours and moments of the day. It could be a word, form of entertainment, even trash on the ground that can set off a knower or invite new fallen to stay and linger.

"The choices they make and the actions that follow live beyond their understanding. If only they knew and could see what we see, would they then change? No. If only they would listen to what's already been taught." Sariel states as he approaches the window to see the true depth of the neighboring fallen.

Across the street and two houses north, he sees Ramiel standing on the porch over his little Emily as she colors on the brick house with chalk. Additionally, and all around the area, it's as if thunderstorms are raging as flashes of light collide with dark, and embers of the fallen scatter to the ground. As if what just took place in Sara's kitchen is happening all over the block. It's a humbling reminder to Sariel that he may be out of DC, but he is not without work. Humbly, he turns and looks back at Sara to reminisce of the day that she was born and the moments that preceded her entry into this world. As if the memory would restore strength and purpose.

Chapter 3

"Sariel, are you excited? Are you ready for this? She's going to be your first. She's going to change some things about you, about how you see, about how you love. It's different when you're involved in their lives and not just writing them down," He says as He places His hand on Sariel's shoulder.

"I'm beyond excited, Master. I have been waiting for this since You created them. I won't let You down, I won't let anything happen to her." Sariel stares into the Master's eyes with a ferocity that can only be the truth.

"I love it. I love your drive and willingness, but I need to explain some things to you before I allow you to go."

"Everything. Please tell me what I need to know to fulfill your word and order. I will do whatever You command."

"She is special. Her name is Sara Adrianne. I created her with my purest love. I took my time when I put her pieces together. I know everything about her, from the number of cells and DNA strands to the number of hairs covering her body for warmth. I know her smile and her heart. I created her soul with such a passion that its brightness would make her sun look like a flame petering to go out. I have put myself into her. She absolutely means very much to me. I need you to understand how precious she truly is."

"I know, Lord, I do. I will watch her as if watching You, nothing will come to harm her—"

"Sariel," the Master interrupts him and places His other hand on his shoulder as if to hold him straight that he may have support for what he is about to hear, "what I'm about to tell you is very difficult, but I need you to understand. I need you to know everything that I have created in her and how it will affect you. I need you to know why."

"Yes, sir, absolutely."

"Sara has been given the gift of choice. The ability to love or not to love, to follow or to stray. She has been given the ability to know good and evil. The curse that her forefather, Adam, put on humanity is still cast down to everyone for all time until my return. It will be her choice whether or not to follow Me.

"They are not created like you were. Your love for Me is beyond wonderful, but it wasn't a choice. You were created to love and to serve Me. Your fallen brothers didn't choose not to love Me anymore, they just choose to believe in the one that said he was my equal. That is why they are so corrupt and angry. I removed my love from them based on that choice.

"However, with Sara, the option is hers. I love her so much that I am allowing her to choose. I want her to choose right, but I won't force the choice again. I won't create creatures of servitude anymore. You and your brothers are all that I will create in that aspect. I love you, and I love them too much to do that again."

"I love You, too, Lord," Sariel interjects as he sees pain begin to form in the eyes of his Master.

"I know you do. The love you have for me is pure and holy and right, but I knew it before you knew Me. The decision that Sara will one day have to make carries the weight of the universe on it. The outcome on both ends is beyond spectacular. To be loved by something that has the ability not to is so moving for Me. It is so pure and righteous, to be loved by one that can choose something else is only matched by my love for them. Do you understand?

"I love her so much that I will allow her to choose her fate when the time comes. But here is where I need you. Here is where I intervene in the slightest way possible. Until that time, until she chooses to be a follower or knower. Until that very moment of knowing, she is under the protection and bloodline of her parents. Her fate is bound with theirs until she chooses. They are her protection until that day. It is their responsibility to choose Me for themselves and for her. I set this law in motion long ago, and it is to remain." The Master drops

His hands from Sariel's shoulders as He clasps them together forming an arrow about to pierce straight through Sariel's being.

"What are you saying? I can't create the barrier as you would have me? I must allow Sara to be subject to them? Her salvation is tied to theirs?" Sariel looks at both parents as they proceed with the birth of their daughter. Her father is to the left of her mother, coaching his wife on with love and support. The room is small and filled with a bed, couch, monitors, one doctor, two nurses, and the parents.

Sariel and the Master watch from above, as if the ceiling were open, and they were monitoring the procedure like medical students. Sara's mother lets out a scream of pain, and the doctor informs her that her baby girl will be here any moment now.

"I can see and know they haven't chosen you yet. How am I to protect her in such an environment?" Sariel asks as he watches Sara get closer and closer to leaving her mother's womb in that hospital room.

"You are to do your very best. The parents are a covering for their family, just like I am covering for mine. Until they choose to follow Me, they are without that covering and protection. Listen, she will be here soon. You will now be allowed to see what I have always seen. Now that you are a protector, your vision of her is as I see her."

Immediately, Sariel's eyes change as his perspective of the young soul alters. Beyond flesh and bone, he sees joy and pure love inside Sara's mother. As if her womb has been replaced with a ball of pure light, her stomach now appears to Sariel as the sun shining in all its glory. Righteous and perfect, Sara's body begins to emerge. As each inch escapes its former occupancy, the image and reflection of light are replaced with darkness and death. The emergence into this world brings the curse of sin and death that Adam and Eve chose so long ago. Her light is now only a glimmer fighting to shine through the tar and stains of that choice that was made for her so long ago.

"Humans quickly forget the responsibility they have chosen and the effects that it has on them and their seed. So many times they chose to be ruled by kings rather than Me, they chose Barabbas rather than Me.

"They forget they were created in my image. I am the Master of creation, responsibility, and order. All of creation was planned and placed in a meticulous fashion. It was not done by accident. They, too, must plan and order their lives. They, too, have choices to make. I am simply letting my creation choose, even though at times it cuts deeper than that cat of nine tails ever could.

I need you, Sariel, to keep guard. You will not be allowed to simply intervene in the human world, your purpose as her protector is to keep the fallen away from her if possible. If they are allowed too much time with her, they will bring her day of knowing sooner and may corrupt her choice. There will be times when you will feel overwhelmed and will fall short of your duty. When this happens, I need you to get back up and continue the fight.

"I chose you specifically for her. Don't leave her until you are told to do so. Her surroundings will come at you like a tidal wave, but I need you to stand firm. She will make mistakes and will be influenced by others, but I need you to never give up. Her parents, until they chose otherwise, will be a hindrance and will bring sorrow. Still, you are not allowed to stop loving her, and you are not allowed to quit. Do you understand?"

"Absolutely I do, Master, and absolutely I will obey."

Sariel recalls that day in his memory as they make their way through the family's nightly routine and eventually tucks Sara into bed. The day he was commissioned to be her protector has been the most significant and most challenging blessing his Master could ever bestow on him. Still, she is worth it, and he has been commanded to protect her, so he will fulfill his duty without hesitation. As Sara closes her eyes to drift asleep, Sariel repeats the words that he spoke that day.

"Absolutely I do, Master, and absolutely I will obey."

Chapter 4

The night ends, and Sara's family wakes. Morning routine ensues, and Bill eventually drives off to work as Nancy and Sara stay inside for a bit as they digest breakfast, and Nancy finishes off the remaining coffee. While all this is transpiring, Sariel keeps a close eye on Sara. He scans back and forth inside the house and out, looking if another attack from the fallen is forming.

The fallen continually make their presence known as one or two come in and out through Nancy as she offers her latest review of other's lives through social media. She's not foaming at the mouth or convulsing, but she is a knower and not a follower, which makes her an open portal. Like a fully gassed-up car, being driven and manipulated without her ever conceiving the idea that she may be used by the enemy.

Besides coming from Nancy, the occasional fallen can be seen making their way through the halls of the home since neither parent has chosen to follow, dropping all defenses except for Sariel. Outside of the house, they continue to litter the streets. Their presence is not as wild and free-flowing now as last night since most parents and children are off to work and school. This is typical behavior for the spiritual world, but Sariel is still on edge even though currently the local numbers of fallen are far fewer. The demonic fallen made their first move last night against his precious Sara, and they are not patient creatures. He knows more will come, over and over again, so he must always be ready.

Eventually, Nancy gets enough of others' fake lives and suggests they head to the park for some fresh air. On the way, Sariel sees Ramiel is already there with Emily and her mom, Becky. Sara also sees Emily and breaks from their pack and heads toward her new friend. Nancy follows and introduces herself to Becky as they approach. They didn't officially meet yesterday, even though the girls did, so they take the next few minutes to get acquainted. They hit it off and begin a long talk of he said, she said.

Sensing that they will be at the park for some time and seeing the danger level is not entirely high at the moment as three other protectors are also in the vicinity, Ramiel and Sariel take this time to go over last night's activities.

"What happened to you last night? When I saw you look at me through the window, I figured something just happened. You looked a little tense and on guard. The large mob of fallen fleeing the scene indicated that something went down. Everything okay, did they get to her?" Ramiel asks as he crosses his arms and braces for the incoming briefing.

"It was nothing, I just introduced myself to the locals, and we had a quick chat. Nothing too big, nothing I couldn't handle. How about you and Emily?" Sariel states as he places his hands on his hips and smirks toward Ramiel.

"You introduced yourself? Hmmm, I know some stuff went down, and yes, you may have talked to them, but what about the details? I want the details. How many did you get last night?" Ramiel asks as he raises his eyebrows in anticipation and tone.

"You want details? Fine, I got forty-seven."

"Forty-seven. That's not a bad number. What caused the commotion?"

"The parents. They were talking in the kitchen while Sara was eating a snack after the park. Nancy started complaining to Bill about the gossip that she heard about them and what people were saying the reason for their move to the suburbs were—"

"How the fallen love to spread their gossip," Ramiel interrupts as he swings his head back, rolls his eyes, and bends his knees to further arch his figure as if hitting a high note.

"Yes, they do. Not even ten seconds into the conversation, they really started to flood in from everywhere. From the windows, through the parents, from the ceiling, they swarmed in to make an impression and to eat it up. It didn't work, I knew something was going to go down as we were walking home, so I was prepared."

"You were prepared? Who told you something was going to happen?"

"The mom, Nancy. She had more fallen following her home last night than normal. Seeing that is always a great sign that something is about to happen."

"Really? I didn't know that."

"You never caught on to that trick? Have you not ever seen that happen before?" Sariel asks puzzled, as if that clue was obvious.

"I guess not, I never really had time to check. Emily's dad, Ralph, is a pervert. So there are always fallen busting at the seams whether he's home or not. It's hard to notice if more follow home or even just show up. I quit counting a couple of years ago and simply expect a full house every day."

"That's rough, I didn't know it could get like that."

"It's not easy, and unfortunately I'm used to it, but she's worth it. Anyway, what else happened? Continue please."

"So, they're filling the whole room, still climbing in from everywhere when it looks like the last one for this battle enters, they begin to speak to me. The voice was loud and skipped across their presence like a rock across a pond. They started saying they were going to make me watch and make her make her decision that night and so on and so forth, you know, all the regular false threats and such. Then after that, I gave them a chance to leave. They didn't, so we battled, and then it was over."

"You gave them a chance to leave? Who does that? I have never heard of a protector doing that before? You're either crazy or you're a saint, my friend. I just go straight in blades swinging. I can't believe you really asked them to leave." Ramiel begins to laugh.

"Well, I'm new to the area. I was trying to be polite."

"Shut your face, that's hilarious. Oh my goodness, I love it." Ramiel takes an arm and nudges Sariel in a joking manner as he continues to laugh. "You were trying to be polite? I'm going to like hanging out with you."

Sariel laughs back before continuing. He didn't realize until after he heard his own story just how ridiculous it honestly sounds.

"Well, we fought for a bit, and I did some damage. Nothing major, but it was fun to flex my wings. They seemed to have had enough when they suddenly stopped, and their scattered voice came back with false threats and empty promises. After that, they left, and I scanned the area and saw you on the porch with Emily. So, what about you, any great or funny story to tell?"

"I don't want to say anything. How can I top that?" Ramiel smirks as he drops his hands to his hips and then looks over at Emily.

"I don't know if you can, but can you at least give me something?"

"Last night was more of the usual. Her mom works as a night nurse, so Ralph was home alone with her. He watches 'inappropriate' things, not even caring if she's in the room or not. He figures she's too young to understand at this point, even though it's not about understanding but exposure. After the night-time dramas, he then puts her to bed and goes to his room and typically watches porn or some crazy movie."

"Well, you must have had a busy night as well."

"Yeah, after we came in from the porch, it all started. Her parents' room shares a wall with hers. She can hear all the noise and moans from Ralph's TV if she's awake. It used to wake her from her sleep and scare her, but sadly, she's gotten used to it. The problem is, his room explodes with fallen so much so that it spills through the walls and into her room. I take care of them when they enter, but it's just annoying. I don't understand the need for any of that filth."

"I don't either. If they only knew what was really happening and the consequences of their actions."

"That's a nice thought, but we both know that wouldn't stop them. Anyway, that's mostly my nightly routine, but I'm used to it, and the fallen are, too. Sometimes I think I hear them complain through the walls before they spill into Emily's room that they don't want to fight anymore. Who knows right?"

"Right." Sariel puts one of his hands to his chin as he thinks about what Ramiel endures on a regular basis.

"So, dad is perverted, and mom is angry about it and is insecure for that reason and others. Both have the usual cocktail of lies, greed, pride, anger, and unforgiveness all wrapped up together. What about your household? What else do Bill and Nancy bring along for the ride?"

"Well, like you said, they too have the usual mix of pride, lying, greed, gossip, anger, and unforgiveness. Nancy has this thing where she gets on her phone and can sit there and just judge and judge people for no reason, then gets mad and makes up arguments in her head with these fake people to justify why she is as she is. Bill either has no backbone or is just tired of arguing, so he just stands around with a drink in hand sipping and listening. Not an authority figure at all, just weak. I believe he drinks to drown her out. It's not a proper response, but it's my theory.

"Besides all of that, they aren't terrible, just your average hypocrite that thinks they are okay because they're good people. They've attended church services for major holidays in the past and believe that no loving god would allow good people to go to hell. You know, the Easter sermon, God loves you and you're fine as you are."

"Oh yeah, mine are hypocrites, too. But hey, speaking of church, have your people picked one out here yet?"

"Not yet, no. Why?"

"I hope you and Sara end up with us at ours. It's actually a good spot. The pastor's not bad, he's a follower, but he could use some spunk in his messages. But we have this group of older women in our church, and they're absolutely awesome. We call them the big five."

"The big five? How do you come up with that for a group name?"

"Well, you would think their protectors were archangels or even cherubim if you saw them. These ladies are freaking prayer warriors. I love going to church because it gives me a break. Plus, their group of warrior angels that accompany their protectors are no small creatures themselves, even though they don't compare to the big five.

"I sometimes just stand back and watch as they clean house. It blows my mind how people still don't follow after having a cleaned out sanctuary. I mean now, we literally make the fallen wait in the parking lot by the dumpsters until the church is out."

"Wow. That is something that I want to see one day. Do the ladies live near here? Maybe I can spot the crew around town." Sariel raises his head to canvass the tops of houses as if he would see giants walking by.

"You probably won't see them around town, they live a decent amount away, and I've only ever seen them at church. But if you can make it, I'll introduce you. You'll like these guys. However, they don't 'ask' the fallen to leave first. Oh, how I can't wait to tell them what you did last night."

Both protectors laugh at what Sariel did and the thought of the conversation that will take place with Ramiel and his church friends this Sunday. He knows this will be one of those stories that will hang around him for at least a millennium. They eventually recompose themselves and continue the conversation.

"Well, I hope I get to meet them one day." Sariel gets a big grin on his face as his mind travels out into the cosmos on the size and force of that group. Eventually, his thoughts are reigned in, and he moves the conversation to local matters. "So, that's good to hear about those ladies and all, but what about this street and neighborhood? How many followers are here? Anything in particular I should be worried about?"

"The Millers, all the way at the north end of the street on my side are followers, and the Pickets on your side of the street are followers. Then there are the Bushbins, Thomas family, and Brown family also on our street, but they live south of us. They're also followers. That's it for our street; it's like that for this entire subdivision really.

"This park is centrally located, and it's the only one for the subdivision, so you will meet most protectors here. However, most of those families I mentioned either don't have kids or the kids have grown and moved away, so you won't really see them except for holidays and such. The Millers and Bushbins were here yesterday, and you saw their protectors for their little ones. But, yeah, that's about it." Ramiel scratches his head as if it would help him think if he is missing anyone else.

"Really? That's it? But there are so many houses. What happened to everyone?"

"Everyone thinks they're a follower. At least that's what they tell themselves or what the 'nice' preacher says. The majority of people don't care anymore. It's not personal as it used to be. It's a fad. Churches have become a hangout and social club or coffee house. It's a talking piece now, like an icebreaker."

"I mean, I knew that's how it was in DC, but I thought out here it would be different. I can't believe it. That's just sad."

"Yeah, it is. So besides that, there aren't any dragons in the area or anything too crazy. If something does come up, it's usually an isolated incident and moves on. Just your average backsliding group of knowers and fallen. Still, there is plenty to do. You'll be busy, but I'm afraid you won't see anything you haven't already seen."

"Well, that part's still good, I guess."

"Sidenote, it looks like the two moms are getting along." Ramiel points to the two women standing and laughing as all four of them watch over their little ones. "Don't let Sara be alone with Emily's dad, Ralph. He hasn't don't anything yet, but the man is not right. He's just covered with too much perversion. I would keep my eye on her around him."

"Absolutely, thanks for the heads-up."

They stay at the park for an additional hour, watching the girls play. Every few minutes the protectors would swat away a fallen that enters their space. During this time, Nancy and Becky exchange contact info and connect online. Sariel and Ramiel continued to chat and stand guard until the ladies separate to go home for lunch. Eventually, the calm of the day ends and the presence of night brings back the knowers that left for work or school. It is just another average day for the humans and another battle for the protectors.

Chapter 5

As a couple of years pass, the same routine ensues: fighting, protecting, watching, and living. The protectors feel the weight of time more heavily now than before. Time is not an issue or condition in heaven. Yet here on earth, Sariel and Ramiel feel every second tick by in its absolute and slow nature. Humanity's limitations are burdensome for protectors as they must never leave their child's side until the day of choosing.

In addition, the neighborhood has seen little change other than the Millers moving away. A family of four knowers took over their residence—mom, dad, and two teenage boys. The Miller warrior angels and protectors will be missed around the park as the heavenly host dwindle down in numbers. Ralph's addiction to lust has become a real problem as his appetite has grown. In fact, the fallen occupying him now are also more significant. His perversion to sexual immorality has fed them well. Nancy has become the street's know-it-all and gossip, which has also caused an increase in size to her inhabitants. Not to the scale of Ralph's entourage, but she has experienced growth nonetheless.

Today, however, is a big day for Emily and Sara. Today, they take the school bus to their very first day of kindergarten. The girls and their parents are beyond excited. This is a big transition for the families. For Sariel and Ramiel, it's a new adventure as well. They haven't been in a public-school setting before other than the young ladies' orientation. At that time, it was a simple walk-through and one on one with the teacher, proposing a small and inadequate scale to what the school will truly be like. However, the simple math for the amount of protectors present will be a nice addition to their two-angel team. They are almost as excited and nervous as the little ladies.

"Oh brother, look at that bus. Do you see that little fallen sitting there? It must be scared out of its mind. It picked the wrong time to manifest from that driver," Ramiel chuckles as he points toward the lone fallen riding the shoulders of the bus driver. Fear and cowardice have caused the creature to shrink to only a bit larger than a garden gnome.

To the human eye, the public school bus is standard sized, seating up to seventy-two. About half of that is occupied by kindergartners, and then there is the lone driver. The children are scattered from the front of the bus to the very back. Each one is wearing a face of excitement, nervousness, anticipation, and thrill. The bus driver is a middle-aged man dressed in the attire of a coach of some kind. It's easy to spot that the smile he has decided to wear is plastered on and not naturally worn. However, to the human eye, the vehicle looks like a happy place to be on its way to the first day of school.

For the spiritual world, it's a little different story. Each child is covered with the presence of their protector. The bus is bursting at its seams with light. There are thunderous conversations going on as protector meets protector. The now-very-small fallen that is occupying the driver is quietly sitting on his shoulders doing his very best not to move. He also has not made a sound, not even a hiss since Sariel and Ramiel have seen the bus arrive. With excitement growing in all of them, the young ladies and their protectors enter the bus. No angel has touched the small creature, the torture of their presence and size is doing more damage to it than their blades ever could.

"Hello everyone," Sariel states as he waves to his new posse members. "I am Sariel, and this is Ramiel. These two little ladies are Emily and Sara."

"Hello," the entire bus erupts as the fellow protectors answer in unison. The crew quickly finds a seat together and sits down. Then the angel closest to them and across the aisle begins to converse with them while the others return to their conversations.

"I am Gadreel, and this little titan of a boy is Robert."

"Hello, Gadreel and Robert," both Sariel and Ramiel answer in unison.

"So, do your girls live on the same block, or is this just their local pickup spot?"

"Emily lives across the street and a couple of homes north of my Sara."

"Wow, that must be nice. My closest protector is over two miles away. Robert's family lives in the country. They decided they wanted their son to go to this public school, so they made arrangements to have him dropped off at the bus stop two spots prior to this. The school will allow it as long as he doesn't miss his bus." As Gadreel finishes his sentence, the bus begins to move to its next destination.

"That's an early morning for the little man. How about for you? Are you on alert through the night or is the country a nice location slim on fallen residency? As you can see here, they occupy a lot of our time, especially at night while knowers have their idle hands and minds," Ramiel points to the exterior of the bus as it passes through wave upon wave of fallen. Like a sea of death, its waves are currently calm but still present and ready to drown its victims.

"Actually, yes, country life is quieter than our current surroundings, yet it has its battles. Robert's mom is a follower while his dad is still a knower. It makes it easier in one aspect as I have additional help at the house.

"But in another light, the father is a drunk. He doesn't hit them physically, but he does emotionally and mentally, which is just as painful. From what I can tell, he's been that way long before Robert was born. He has twenty-two rather large fallen occupying him in addition to the usual stragglers that use him as a portal. We've had some close calls with them and Robert, but we have persevered. How about you two? How are the suburbs?" Gadreel asks eagerly to learn of suburban life.

"Do you want to answer this one or me?" Ramiel asks as he turns to Sariel.

"You can handle this, I will just listen and correct you if needed," Sariel chuckles as he nudges his friend to begin.

"Thank you for your permission," Ramiel smiles and then returns back to Gadreel. "It is a daily fight for us. More so at night than during the day. We occasionally have a skirmish or two during the day, but typically it's quiet. Most knowers have either left for work or school, taking legions of fallen with them.

"My Emily's dad is overwhelmed with lust and sexual perversion. He has several large fallen dwellers, but not twenty-two. However, other fallen use him as a highway to come and go, so his presence is littered with them continually. Sara's mom is the local gossip and also has several large inhabitants. Both of our other parents simply exist and conform to their partners. Almost accepting their problems as a remedy to not being alone.

"Every night, a battle takes place. We've had a couple of close calls. For me in particular, the first night the larger fallen appeared, I was thrown off guard. I didn't expect it, so they were able to get a few seconds with Emily. I was beyond angry and eventually broke free from their grasps. That night, in particular, I took out 437 fallen. I never want to feel that again, and I pray I never will." Ramiel lowers his head as the memory finishes running its course. Sariel notices his friend's moment of guilt and offers solace with an interjection.

"I had a similar experience, almost word-for-word to Ramiel's story. It lasted long enough to set a standard to never allow it to happen again. The attacks continue to happen, and we continue to stand, praise be to the Master."

"Praise be to the Master," Gadreel and Ramiel reply in unison.

"I have never experienced anything like that, and I am thankful I hadn't. It makes a huge difference when you have help. Those three warrior angels and her protector are a force to be reckoned with. The five of us are a solid team, and we work together as much as possible. The benefit in Robert's mom is she is pretty much hip to hip with him when he's home, so we move like one unit."

"That must be nice. We don't have that. Now there is a park centrally located in our subdivision, and we get a break when all the children are playing because of our numbers. But for Sariel and I, and most of the other protectors in our area, at night the job is lonesome."

The bus comes to a stop, and the protectors take the opportunity to gather their surroundings. They see they are now only a couple of blocks away from their destination as a sizeable directional school sign points toward the parent drop-off area. The bus begins to move again as quickly as it stopped. Following the signs and taking one last left turn, they finally reach the parking lot area of the school. The entirety of the school comes into full view within moments of passing over a speed bump in the drop-off zone.

To the human eye, it is a nicely designed and clean elementary school all on one level. In the spiritual realm, it is a fortress covered from top to bottom with protectors, messenger angels, and warrior angels. Beyond them and surrounding the entire school, except the unloading area, are legions upon legions of fallen. As the school bus approaches and its doors open, the sound is a deafening roar of hate, love, victory, loss, and combat. The protectors all glance at each other as if to make sure each one sees what the other is. It appears almost like a volcano of death is spewing out fallen from the track field east of their location. The enemy presents itself to form a wall of lava-like death, engulfing everything they come into contact with.

As angel's exit the bus, the little fallen that wouldn't move a muscle just moments earlier is now cackling as they pass by on their way out. As if the sight and presence of his brethren give him a false sense of hope. The protectors line the sidewalk with their little ones and stand in awe, mouths shut and eyes wide open. This school is a war zone, and the battle is raging. It's a massive and unwelcome reminder of the great force their enemy presents.

Sariel breaks his glance from the moving canvass of war and looks toward his brothers. He takes two steps to the side and out of their line, positioning himself that the other protectors will see him and give him their attention.

"Absolutely I will obey, Master!" he shouts for his war cry as he lifts both blades from his hips igniting them as they ascend and activating his entire armor set.

"Absolutely I will obey, Master!" all of the other protector's shout in unison as they follow his actions and leadership.

The battle for their kindergarteners has begun.

31

Chapter 6

"Form wall, protectors!" Grigori shouts as he stands center mass in the middle of Ms. Johnson's classroom. Each protector begins to move and stand shoulder to shoulder with their brothers presenting themselves, as if the redwoods outside of San Francisco decided to create a barrier. Swords out and at the ready, the wall of light is further exhuming its shine as each sword is covered in fire at its purest form. Their armor presents itself to the looking eye as a newly constructed skyscraper of metal and enormity. Layers of flat skillfully crafted armor are woven together by chain mail and metallic links. The fire from the swords reflects off the armor and pierces the eyes of an onlooker like the morning sun crashing through the windshields of vehicles headed east.

"Wings out!" Grigori orders as he issues another command. Upon the utterance of the final syllable, each wing opens, left and right, causing the protectors to move forward just to create the space necessary for their wingspans. Because the armor of the angels is in full effect, so are their wings. Each feather is covered in the same metallic fashion and material that encompass the armor set. This transforms these small creations of soft and silky flight to individual spears of death and power. As if they converted from eagle's wings to the wingspan of the world's deadliest fighter jet.

Each protector that was on that bus chatting and acquainting themselves with each other are now side by side in a perfect formation all around the classroom. Their demeanor and attitude have shifted to complete obedience, with the only acceptable outcome being a victory. To the human eye, they stand and look as if they are lining the classroom walls. In the spiritual realm, the walls have vanished, and the battlefield is beyond the classroom. As the protectors are linked by the formation, their vision has altered that they may be able to see the scope of what's in front of them.

Legions is not a word large enough to describe the enemy that is forming around the campus. Black death is what's visible as the fallen numbers are so large that it appears to be one mass. One sea mass that rocks and swings closer toward the classrooms in the facility.

The waves glisten as red and yellow eyes open and close, causing a similar effect as when the sun shines off of the ocean's wave. The stench of death cannot only be smelled by all, but can also be seen as clouds of gas erupt from their formation as the bodies rise and fall in unison, as if dancing to the same drum. Shards of cheap metal also reflect off of their presence as its faded silver tone stands out and away from the black wave of death. The cry of the enemy is beyond vulgar. It is a curse of absolute hatred. The center mass of this tidal wave begins to rise as a lone fallen stand above the rest, positioning himself as commander. His size is that of a grizzly bear on steroids. He is not a beast to be tamed or taken for granted. His sword more resembles the size of a spear than a sword. Its covering is tar, and death as blackness drips from its hilt.

"Listen to me, protectors, and we will have victory here this day." Grigori shouts, bringing the attention off of the fallen and toward him as he prepares the angels for the onslaught of the enemy. "Do not waver, and do not move from your position, regardless of what may happen around you or your little one."

Immediately, Sariel and Ramiel remember both Emily and Sara and turn their heads to look at their little ladies. They are playing with the other children on the rug that is in the center of the classroom. There is peace around the children as they interact one with another, oblivious to what is happening around them. All of their desks are lined in rows at the center of the room. Their cubbies line half of the wall, while cabinets full of toys, books, and craft items cover the remaining sections of the wall. The teacher's desk is at the head of the class in its center, and behind it is a screen and mounted projector coming from the ceiling. Scattered throughout the room are pockets of play areas for the children. Each area, as well as the entire room, sings with color as each desk, cubby, and cabinet are covered in bright and loud colors.

"Eyes front, protectors!" Grigori commands with a shout of authority and intolerance. "For your little ones to survive this day, we must work as one. Each protector is one protector for the entire class. On this field, there is no individual more important than the rest. To believe and act on that premonition would bring defeat, and that is not allowed. Do you understand?"

"Yes, sir!" each protector shouts as their gaze and attention return to the sea of incoming death.

"My name is Grigori, and I am the messenger angel assigned to Ms. Johnson's classroom. You will follow my commands as I issue them. Do not hesitate and do not evaluate. I see all that is happening, and I command all to react in the same manner. I know the enemy's plans and how to stop them. To trust me is to trust the Master that sent me. Understood?"

"Yes, sir!" all protectors shout as one voice.

"In addition to you, we also have eleven warrior angels to handle any and all fallen that make their way beyond your wall. They also are assigned to this classroom until the Master tells them otherwise. Your new job, protectors, is simple. Do as I say and work together."

Behind their wall are massive warrior angels. They are all at least ten feet tall with wingspans of twenty feet. Their armor is as majestic as the protectors, as well as their swords. Everything is like for like between the groups, except for the size. These angels tower over everything.

One of the warrior angels is fixated on Ms. Johnson, a knower, and has his two blades piercing through her soul, causing her portal to be shut. This will stop the fallen from using her as a backdoor through their defense. The messenger angel is in the center. He is not as tall as the warrior angels, but he is still a substantial being. His armor is light, and he only carries one sword in hand. The other hand is filled with a horn, used for signaling the group and others on campus.

After a few moments, the wave begins to pick up speed. It becomes an earthquake of death as it starts toward the classroom, causing everything spiritual to feel the shake of its enormity. The protector angels lower their legs and raise their arms up and out to help brace for the incoming impact.

"Finally, my brethren, be strong in the Lord, and in the power of his might." As Grigori shouts, all of the angels in the room join in with one accord. They have a voice of triumph as they finish the passage with such a force that it causes the realm to shake even more: "Put on the whole armor of God, that ye may be able to stand against the wiles of the devil. For we wrestle not against flesh and blood, but against principalities, against powers, against the rulers of the darkness of this world, against spiritual wickedness in high places. Wherefore take unto you the whole armour of God, that ye may be able to withstand in the evil day, and having done all, to stand. Stand therefore, having your loins girt about with truth, and having on the breastplate of righteousness. And your feet shod with the preparation of the gospel of peace. Above all, taking the shield of faith, wherewith ye shall be able to quench all the fiery darts of the wicked. And take the helmet of salvation, and the sword of the Spirit, which is the word of God: Praying always with all prayer and supplication in the Spirit, and watching thereunto with all perseverance and supplication for all saints."

As soon as they finish shouting, darkness crashes against them like waves of the ocean wrapping around a cliffside and shooting into the air. The sound of the collision is only matched by a volcanic eruption with a scale of nine or higher. The fallen sink into each other as they meet the immovable wall. Each protector is keeping his arms out, merely bracing and withstanding the option of collapse. The fallen quickly adapt and use each other to climb over the wall of protectors, trying to find a way inside their circle and disrupt their formation.

As they leap off one another and over the protectors, they are met with the blades of the warrior angels. Sariel and Ramiel look up and see fiery and sharp tree trunks swing with ease and grace and connect with each fallen. The trees are quickly realized to be blades as they slice without mercy through the enemy. As the wave continues to crash against the shore of protectors and the warriors continue to keep the skies clear of any fallen, Grigori takes his horn and gives three fast bursts. Immediately the wings of the protectors bend and twist facing the fallen. With another quick blast of his horn, all of the protector's spin with a complete 360-degree turn, slicing and destroying every fallen they come in contact with. This move gives the angels less than a second break, but its effect is powerful. Still, the fallen crash again against their wall, not missing a step. The number of fallen is still beyond counting as their wave finds the shore again.

The fallen are not idiots and have a plan of their own. Their lead commander screams profanity into the air, and his legions react accordingly. Their waves continue to crash against the protectors, but the fallen further back begin to throw ropes with hooks attached to them at the wall. This is not meant to scale the wall, but instead act as a hook to catch and reel in a protector. Twenty of these objects land behind the angelic wall. Without hesitation, the closest warrior angel swipes with his blade and cuts their rope. He is able to get all of them except two. The fallen immediately begin to pull and the two not cut find the backs of two protectors. One of these angels is Ramiel. As the rope is pulled, the hooks sink deep in his back right where his wings protrude from his body. He roars like a lion as the hooks sink even deeper, and he feels himself begin to lift off the ground. Almost as quickly as that happens, Grigori gives his horn two blasts. This time, the sound lingers more prolonged than the prior bursts. As soon as the last note leaves the horn, a squadron of angels instantly fly down from the heavens and cut the ropes pulling on the two protectors. They vanish just as fast as they appeared, like they were fighter jets waiting in the clouds for orders.

Again and again, this dance of light and dark continues. The fallen continue to press, and the protectors continue to resist. Eventually, the battle calms as the third, fourth, and fifth graders are sent outside for recess. This causes the fallen to focus their attention on the other children, giving this kindergarten class of protectors a much-needed break. The warrior angels that were once in the center of the group leave to go join the other groups of angels that are battling outside. The messenger angel and protectors stay for nap time. As they have this break, Sariel approaches Grigori with some questions.

"How much time do we have until they come back?"

"Typically, recess and nap time are thirty minutes."

"Why is this happening, I never knew it was like this at school. I was actually excited to come here today. Is this happening every day?" Sariel asks with a sense and look of disappointing amazement.

"This is your day now for 300 plus days a year until your child's time of choosing. School is a battleground," Grigori replies without hesitation, as if this is nothing new for him.

"How can this be? Why does the enemy have a such a presence here?"

"Do you not remember what happened the year of 1962? This nation removed prayer from their schools. The following year they removed the Bible, and by 1980 the Ten Commandments were removed. This has been a war zone for a long time, even before those dates. The difference being before that time, the battles were easier for us. This nation doesn't want our Master here, it's that simple."

Grigori returns to watching the battle that's taking place on the playground and Sariel returns to Ramiel. He humbly thinks on what has happened over the years as he checks on his friend's back to see if there is any real damage. He whispers a prayer of healing to heal and restore any damage that was done. As he finishes his prayer, he is taken back by the recollection of different incidents that have happened on earth through the years. He turns to watch Sara sleep as she lay on her hammock. He bends on one knee and kisses her forehead. As he is doing this, Grigori blows his horn, signaling that recess is wrapping up, and the battle will begin again shortly. Before Sariel rises, he whispers into Sara's ear.

"I love you so much. The Master loves you so much. Please choose the Master."

Chapter 7

Two years pass since that first day of kindergarten—two years of battle, stress, growth, and hard work. Quickly, however, the classroom confrontations become a welcoming sight compared to the fights at home alone. It is a pleasure and relief for Ramiel and Sariel to fight alongside each other, as well as the additional angels, compared to battling at home alone. Now towering over eight feet apiece, they have grown just as their little ones have. Both in wisdom and in size, Ramiel and Sariel are not the same small protectors that they started out to be.

This past summer, Sara's mom, Nancy, was invited by Becky, Emily's mom, to a ladies-night-out church group. Surprisingly, she enjoyed herself immensely as they all clicked and got along rather well. While they were at dinner, one of the moms from church invited their family to attend. Of course, the other ladies chimed in, and all said it would be lovely for their family to go and to hang out with them on Sundays. Happily, Nancy agreed, and that brings us to this morning. Today marks the first day that the family will be attending church together, outside of holidays and special events, since their empty dedication of Sara as a newborn.

Ramiel is beyond excited that his friend will be joining him; Sariel feels the same. In addition to being at church, Sariel wants to finally see these massive angels that Ramiel has been speaking of. His latest statement is that there really isn't a battle at church anymore, the fallen merely wait in the parking lot. Few dare try to disrupt the service anymore, and some unaware and unfortunate fallen make the mistake of using a knower as a portal exit.

Every so often, there is a celebration as a knower becomes a follower. When this happens, the angels present and on high all erupt.

The Master Himself is there for the process, and a party like no other ensues. Sariel is hoping that such a party happens today for the members of his family. If not for Sara, at least for her parents that they may provide support and additional protection for her and themselves. Sara is still under their authority until her moment of choosing; and until that time, their salvation covers hers as well.

Slowly and almost begrudgingly, the family wakes and gets dressed for the new occasion. Sariel jumps, swings his blades, and shouts at all fallen that may try to delay this event from happening. He works overtime as he flashes between parents and child, seeing how much longer before they hit the road. Eventually, all come together, and the family is on their way. Sariel rides atop the vehicle and is radiant with joy as they head toward the church. Tears of joy begin to overwhelm him as each tire rotation further speeds the journey along.

As they get closer, Sariel is startled as he notices the top of a building begin to shift back and forth as it appears to inch north. Moments later four additional buildings seem to move. He stands as high as he can on the moving vehicle, not thrown or off balance, to see what is going on. He places his hands on his blades, preparing for trouble, when all of a sudden, he sees wings flutter as if a breeze has blown through them.

"Those are angels?" Sariel gasps as his right hand goes from hip to straight out as it points toward the moving structures. Outside of seeing archangels, Sariel can't recall seeing angels this massive before. The vehicle pulls into the parking lot, and the monstrosity of size is now set before him. Each angel is slightly taller than the height of the church building as they all tower over thirty feet and more. The armor is an exact copy of the protector's, only amplified tenfold. The majesty of such metal and power is breathtaking to any and all creatures, spirit or mortal. He continues to stand on top of the car with his hand still pointed at them as the vehicle parks. As the family unbuckles, Sariel hasn't moved an inch as he has yet to break his gaze from these creatures.

"What did I tell you? They're big, huh?" Ramiel chuckles as he speaks to his stunned friend. "You, sir, are about to get a much-needed break." Ramiel then motions for his friend to come toward the entrance.

By this time Sara and her parents have exited the car. Sara sees Emily and runs toward her, ignoring her parents' command of caution through the parking lot. Sariel finally breaks his gaze as he joins Bill and Nancy to catch up and meet with Emily, Nancy, and Ramiel at the entrance. The family is greeted at the door, hugged and handed information about the church on a pamphlet.

"Where's the dad?" Sariel asks as he looks back up at the giants.

"Hey buddy, down here, okay. Down here real quick. Dad doesn't come, he knows what he is, and he'd rather watch the game or sleep in." Ramiel snaps his fingers to bring his friend's attention toward himself as he finishes speaking.

"Sorry. It's hard not to stare. I just haven't seen one so big since being here, not even in DC. You are correct that these guys are impressively large," Sariel chuckles as he rubs the back of his head, hoping it would help him grasp their size.

"Oh yeah, you think that's impressive? Look over there." Ramiel points toward the back of the parking lot near the church dumpsters.

Following his finger, Sariel sees hordes of fallen. They're hissing and shouting curses toward the church, but not a single one of them makes a move beyond the dumpster. As if an invisible barrier has been set for the fallen that they won't cross.

"I haven't seen power like that in quite some time. What's causing them to stay back?" Sariel continues his astonishment as he sees the fallen corralled like cattle in a pen.

"That, sir, is because of them," Ramiel then points inside the church to a group of five older ladies that are sitting together. "Three of them are sisters, and the other two are cousins. They have been followers since the time of choosing. They all chose on the same night at the same service. They are warriors, and their squad of protectors and warrior angels reflect it. In fact, those clusters of angels inside are the warriors for them. It's not very often you see warrior angels smaller than protectors. Isn't that awesome?" Ramiel is electrified as he speaks.

"Wow!" Sariel is in astonishment as he continues to absorb his new surroundings. "This almost feels like home."

"Yes, it does, my friend. Yes, it does."

Eventually, the greeting ends and the two families head inside. Sara and her parents sit toward the back with Emily and her mom. Not all the way back, but the beginning of the end section. Just far enough to not be called upon, but also not far enough to think any less of them. The church entrance is a large foyer roughly thirty yards long and twenty yards wide with restrooms on each side, tables covered in pamphlets, motivational material, a coffee and snack area, and greeters. Just before reaching the doors entering the sanctuary, there is a hallway to the right that leads to Sunday school classes and a nursery.

The auditorium itself is massive. Its ceilings are twenty-five feet tall, and its depth is equal to a football field. Rows and rows of pews line both sides of the area as a center aisle has been made from their absence. The center stage is covered in musical equipment and a podium. Behind that is the baptismal tank.

The warrior angels take spots at each exit of the auditorium, two on each door. One door in the front of the church to the left behind the baptismal that is displayed in the center of the wall. The two doors that are the main entrance and exit of the facility. And two additional entries that are located near the nursery and children's section of the church. The remaining warriors patrol back and forth, but mainly walk and talk as no patrol is genuinely needed.

By this time, the five gigantic and massive protector angels have sat Indian style surrounding the auditorium. Their beings push beyond the threshold of the interior and exterior walls. The tops of their wings where the metacarpus bends down are present, but the remaining structure hides outside beyond the church walls. There are other angels also present in the sanctuary. Several other families and family members are followers, but their entourage simply doesn't match. In fact, the pastor's own squad of protection is not on par with the five ladies seated up front.

"Hey everyone, this is my friend Sariel that I was telling you about." Ramiel side hugs his friend as he grins, as if he were holding a favorite toy and presenting it at show-and-tell.

"Hello, Sariel," everyone answers.

"Hello," Sariel excitedly greets the group, "it's great to be here. I've heard a lot about you all, and I am thrilled to say that the stories don't do you justice." Not an embarrassed type of excitement, but rather bashfulness as he is thoroughly impressed.

"Come on, don't do that. Their heads will actually get bigger if you talk to them like that," Jequn replies as he nudges one of the massive protectors. Everyone laughs and nods, the group is used to the attention being on their building-sized protectors.

The laughter continues, but Sariel is interrupted as he hears a thunderous explosion outside, as if a swift gust of hurricane force winds had gone screaming by. He turns his gaze toward the door and places both hands on his blades, changing from bashful to prepared. In doing so, his new companions and friends laugh even more at his quick gesture.

"What's so funny? Didn't you hear that? There could be an attack forming." Sariel circles in place to see what everyone else is doing. He notices that not even one of the patrolling warrior angels has moved toward the sound. No one, in fact, has reacted or even twitched toward the explosive wind. The only change has been their laughter toward him.

"Relax, my friend," Ramiel puts his hands on Sariel's shoulders to calm him. "That was nothing. Actually, if you wait a few more seconds, you will definitely hear it again." Within seconds another thunderous eruption occurs. "That is the sound of that protector having a little fun," Ramiel points to the behemoth protector that is sitting closest to the entry doors of the church.

"His wings are swatting away any fallen that dare walk by the front doors. Sometimes, they aren't paying attention to their sur-roundings as they are busy distracting their knower. Suddenly and without warning, they get the ride of the century that they never asked for." As Ramiel finishes his statement, another thunderous sound cracks. Sariel looks up at the protector who, in return, looks down on him and gives him a wink.

"Oh my goodness, that's uh… that's one of… that is simply—"

"We know. You'll get used to it as well. We all still laugh a little internally every time we hear it, but we've been listening to it for some time now, so we're used to it."

"Wow!" Sariel's mouth drops open as he gazes beyond the wall and into the street to watch it occur.

"Wow is right."

The group chuckles a little more and then begins to converse and hang out as the protection duties are mainly filled by the big five.

"Hello, I'm Jequn. Who do you have the pleasure of protecting here today?" Jequn asks Sariel as he comes to greet the new guest.

"I'm with that little lady right there," Sariel points to Sara as the congregation is now singing and clapping to the praise music.

"She's beautiful, my friend."

"Thanks. She truly is. And how about you, who are you with?"

"I am with that man right there," Jequn points toward the pastor as he tries to clap on beat.

"Wow, good for you. You must be busy," Sariel raises both eyebrows and cheekbones as he looks toward the pastor.

"Yes, we are, but you are as well, according to Ramiel."

"There's never a dull moment, but I do like this break we're having right now."

"It's nice to work together and to see the body perform as one, like it was intended."

"That's exactly right. Speaking of the body, how is the congregation here?" Sariel looks around at all those in attendance.

"It's still a chore. The fallen that inhabit those that attend here wait outside, and the stupid few that use a knower as a portal quickly travel back through if they are paying attention, and we don't greet them fast enough ourselves. A lot of our work has changed to outside of this place. We have a smart enemy who has adapted to our body here and all over the world, so it caused us to adapt as well."

"What do you mean? What's going on? What's the problem now?" Sariel asks for the joy that once resided on his face has now been evicted by contemplation.

"The enemy, unless scaling a large attack, doesn't really stand a chance in here if you can see by our presence. However, don't let us fool you. We are fewer than you are allowing your eyes to accept." Jequn places one hand on Sariel's shoulder and begins to turn in a 360-degree motion to show the actuality of the congregation.

"I know our massive friends are just that, massive, but how many others do you see? Beyond them and their warrior campanions, beyond the protectors of the young ones and my squad for the pastor, how many other angels do you see? I will tell you. The answer is sixty-eight. Sixty-eight other angels congregate here with us today. That means that there are seventeen other believers besides the big five and my pastor. Now, how many people do you believe are in attendance today?"

"I would say over or between 200 to 220 with a quick scan," Sariel humbly states the number as he understands what his new friend is continuing to explain.

"There are 211 in service today. That leaves us with about eleven percent of the congregation, including the pastor, as followers. Don't let the additional protectors distract you, there aren't that many followers here today. You're new, so I will tell you about our conniving and smart enemy. Look around and what do you see in the laps of most of these people?"

Sariel scans the audience and looks for what was asked of him. "Phones. I see their phones out."

"Now look at those people and see who is using that phone to access the Word or for other entertainment."

Sariel notices only two people using the phone with the Word on its display.

"They are distracted. Life is more important to many of them on that phone than the one they are currently living. They are making appointments, lunch reservations, chatting with friends, playing games or watching videos. They are living in the future and not the now. They are not guaranteed that time, but are told by the enemy to worry about the Master later and live for themselves now, even though they are consumed by the false future.

"They think that the device is showing them their current life, but it's just a distraction for a later time. People use it for shallow self-gratification and a false acceptance. How many likes or heart-shaped icons will their post have at the end of the day? How many shares or comments. Too many times, people use those things to document their now for false future praise, but they miss out on what's in front of them.

"Even outside of the church, just at parks or a gathering of friends, they miss the glorious creation set before them for a false sense of acceptance or depression. Besides those phones, we have other knowers that are either talking to their neighbor"—Jequn points to Sara and Emily's moms—"daydreaming, or are here as a social club, a rite of passage, and mediocre hangout. It's a place to go on Sunday because that's what their relatives did before them. However, beyond that mess, beyond the phones and plans and coffee cups, beyond the social recognition and the social media mockery of checking into the church, there are a few that are actually listening. The listeners are fascinating to watch," Jequn points to a specific couple that is intently listening to the word being presented to them.

Sariel leans forward, as if to get a better look. Those humans are entirely engaged with the pastor as their body language would suggest that his words were their oxygen. They provide their full attention, soaking in everything that is being taught, regardless of any distraction from their surroundings. It's as if he can see the words enter into them and digest into their being, providing the spiritual nutrients their soul longs for.

"They are lucky because they are in a church where truth is actually taught and not just self-promotion or self-wealth and health. If you listen closely, you can hear the Master call to them and urge them to take His hand. To choose Him. 'But why aren't they doing it?' you might ask. What's wrong?"

"I don't know," Sariel states as he takes in the process that is happening before his eyes.

"He won't force them. You can clearly see they are listening, learning, and it's exciting to watch, but the decision is entirely on them. They were created to be able to choose for themselves. If they do choose to follow, when that moment occurs, and they begin to believe and start the process, it's like nothing else you've seen.

"When they come to repentance, thousands of angels appear and erupt with such joy. The celebration is beyond their realm of understanding. Then, after they have accepted the Master and follow His plan set out in His word, then another eruption occurs and proceeds the previous one a hundredfold. The Master Himself appears and greets their spirit and cleanses it as they rise from the water. 'On that day, you will know that I am in my Father, and you in Me, and I in you.'"

"I want to see that. Is that going to happen today?" Sariel looks to Jequn as an excited young child would listen to a parent for approval.

"I pray it does every day and every service. But it's up to them. He won't choose for them like He did with us. They have the right of choice. I think that's why it's such a big deal for Him. They can choose whatever they want and, on those days, they choose Him. It truly is breathtaking to witness."

Sariel and Jequn finish talking, and Sariel goes over to stand behind Sara. He takes in the crowd as he watches over her shoulder. Excitement and sadness sweep through him like waves crashing against the shore as the words from his new friend replay in his thoughts. He is heartbroken for all those in attendance not taking advantage of the opportunity before them. He is excited that Sara has the chance to hear the Master's words for the first time and possibly choose Him.

Sariel's body begins to motion like a roller coaster, up and down as he checks on Sara to see if she understands what is happening and what is being said; to see if she comprehends the talking points presented by the pastor. Unfortunately, she is talking and playing with Emily as their mothers also speak and interact with each other and their phones, showing their daughters the examples of mannerism at church. It only takes a word—a spark—to ignite the process of choice and acceptance. As long as Sara's parents are knowers and not followers, then she is subject to their destination as well. Sariel prays for his little Sara to come to her own understanding.

"Please, Sara, please listen. One day, when choice first presents itself, you will have to make your own decision. Please choose the Master."

Sariel humbly stops the rise and fall actions and stands guard for the remainder of the service. Not for an attack, but for the possible time of choosing, as if today could be the day. The other angels know what he is doing, they sense his contemplation and give him his space. However, each of them glances over at him through the remainder of the service and offer a nod of support and love. They understand what he is experiencing and seeing for the first time. The highs and lows of watching, waiting, and protecting.

Chapter 8

Months have passed and with them the summer. School started six weeks ago, as well as the familiar routine of fighting and protecting as before. The difference with each year is that as the children move up in their grade, so do the fallen. Each year, the fallen have grown larger and harder to combat. Whether it's the curriculum or the advanced age and ideas that are causing the fallen to grow, the battles intensify as Sara and Emily get older. The girls are only in the third grade, but the job required to protect them is not elementary.

Tonight marks another milestone in the lives of Emily and Sara, as well as Ramiel and Sariel. Tonight is the first ever sleepover for these young ladies. Nancy has taken the burden of entertainer and host. Sara and Becky must journey far as they cross the street and go two homes north to reach their destination. This is one of the few Friday nights that Nancy actually has off, and she wanted to spend it with her daughter. When Emily was asked what she wanted to do for the evening, she stated that she wanted to have Sara over and the three of them to have a makeup party and sleepover. The parents agreed, and that is what brings them together this evening.

"Are you excited?" Becky asks, looking down at Sara as they reach the front lawn.

"Yeah, we're going to have a makeup party and do our nails and stuff. I'm going to look fly." Sara whips her hair off of her shoulders as she closes her eyes and quickly poses for the nonexistent camera.

"You're going to have so much fun, and you always look beautiful to me." She leans down and kisses the top of Sara's head. "You're just growing up on me, aren't you? You're my big girl."

"Come on, mom, I'm not a big girl. I'm a grown kid now. I'm in the third grade. I'm not little anymore. I don't talk like a little girl. I'm mature now. I even have a boyfriend."

Sariel rolls his eyes and squeezes his blade handles a little firmer as he recalls Jackson Montgomery, a young man in Sara's class that told her that he liked her after tripping her during recess. *That young man is not worthy of my Sara. He's foolish, rude, and mean. He does not qualify for her, now or maybe ever,* Sariel's thoughts continue to cast judgment against the absent young man until they arrive at their friend's front door, and Nancy begins to ring the doorbell.

"Listen to me, Sara, before you go inside. You must listen and do what Emily's parents say, okay? They are in charge tonight."

"I know, I will. But if I get scared or if anything happens, can I come home?" Sara asks as she hugs her mother's leg for stability and support as she realizes she will be leaving momentarily.

"Of course, my love. We're just right there across the street. I know you're nervous, but you're going to have a great time tonight. I've been told that you are going to give each other manicures, pedicures, and do each other's makeup and hair. I'm actually really jealous. It sounds like it's going to be a blast."

"What's a manocore?" Sara butchers the pronunciation as she looks up at her mother, releasing her grip on her leg.

"Manicures and pedicures are hand and feet makeup stuff."

"Oh, gotcha. That's right. Yeah, those are going to be great."

Becky reaches at the front door and swings it open as wide as possible without hitting the wall behind it. Sara and Nancy begin to laugh and smile as the open door reveals the outrageous and loud attire that Becky has greeted them in. She is dressed from head to toe as an '80s hipster with wild makeup, plastic jewelry, and big fluffy baggy clothes.

"Oh my god. Like, come on inside, you guys. Like, this is going to be totally rad, you know?" She barely is able to finish her sentence with her fake California-girl accent before she also bursts into laughter, joining her guests.

"Girl, you look amazing," Nancy states as she looks her up and down in awe.

"Thank you, thank you," She poses in multiple positions while replying.

Both moms then embrace for a hug as Sara slips past them and heads toward Emily's room. Sariel is also laughing as he hopes that Ramiel is in similar fashion for the evening. Sariel purposely follows Sara slowly inside so he can try to catch the end of the mom's conversation before they part ways.

"I'm home for the night, so I will be with the girls. We're going to play and be silly and have lots of fun. I'm actually looking forward to tonight and to be silly."

"If this is any indication of what's to come, I may have to go grab a bag and sleep here as well. You three are going to have a riot," They both laugh.

"You totally should."

"I want to, and I would, but we have 'special' plans for tonight, and I'm not allowed to miss it. It's been a while for Bill, and I need to be nice," She winks and smirks while smiling from ear to ear.

"Oh well, you better run home, do your duty, grab your bag, and come on back. We will see you soon, right? What do you say, about fifteen minutes before you're back?"

"Girl, you are too much. You know it won't even take that long," both ladies bend over in laughter as they take a few seconds to compose themselves before departing. "Listen, if she acts up or needs anything, just text me or call me."

"Absolutely! You know I will, but she will be fine. The girls are so easy because they get along so well. Plus, Ralph will spend most of his night in our room, sleeping or watching a movie. He had a busy day, so I imagine about twenty minutes after pizza, he'll be out. It's easy when the girls are the only two children I have to watch."

"You are too much. Hey, if you get any good shots or something funny happens, would you post it and tag me with it online, so I can see as well?"

"Of course, of course, I will. Now go get to work. Your man needs you."

"Thanks again, we really do appreciate it."

Both ladies hug and then separate as one closes the door and the other heads back home.

"What a disappointment," Sariel shakes his head as he enters Emily's bedroom and looks over his friend.

"What's wrong, what happened?" Ramiel asks as he searches for a problem.

"I was hoping you would be dressed up as well, like her mom. I was picturing you covered in makeup and your hair styled in pretty bows and your nails sparkling with some color of glitter."

"You know that actually sounds pretty nice, and I think I could pull it off with the right colors," Ramiel sarcastically replies as he catches his friend's joke.

Both angels laugh and embrace. Now all four of them are in Emily's bedroom as the protectors stand in the middle of the room glancing around for any type of activity. The bedroom is covered from floor to ceiling in different shades of pink. Emily's bed is in the corner furthest from the door, and her dresser is on the opposing wall. This creates the most space to allow dancing, playing, and other activities. Clothes and shoes litter the floor, as well as old makeup kits and stuffed animals.

"So, what do you think we can expect tonight? Calm night or busy?" Sariel asks since this is his first overnight with Ramiel as well as Sara with Emily.

"Well, it looks promising, but that could all change. Becky is still a knower, but she's actually pretty calm. Mostly, fallen use her as a portal for entry on days like today. She typically is swamped with them after work, but she's been home all day, so they haven't clung on to her.

"The dad is probably going to fall asleep after dinner since he had a busy day working on-site. The benefit of his construction job is that sometimes he's just too tired to do anything. Now, he still has the fallen that occupy him and the others that use him as a portal, but the occupants stay with him like we do with the girls. If he can stay asleep and the mom doesn't get called into work, it should end up being a standard or maybe even a calm night."

"Well, that sounds great," Sariel stretches his arms and wings out as far as possible, as if preparing to relax.

"Hey, do you think your family may come to church more often? It's always great seeing you, and the other guys really like you as well."

"I would love to, but you know it's not me or Sara to decide but her parents. They like to sleep in and stay up late the night before. Although they seem to enjoy themselves when they go, I know I do. It's just not always convenient for them. There's always something going on, or they have a trip to take somewhere. It's just not a priority."

"I know, I hear it all the time from other angels as well. The good thing about Emily's mom is that she goes pretty regularly. She uses it as a break from work and from Emily. It's her time to sit, have her coffee, and catch up on social media while someone else watches her kid. It also gives her a break from her husband. He still doesn't attend."

"How is that going by the way? Are they doing any better?" Sariel asks, knowing they have been having some issues lately.

"Not really. They don't even really argue about his porn addiction anymore. It's become too much of a hassle, so they both just ignore it. She's over it and him, but he won't get help or counseling, so she just grows more and more miserable. He doesn't think it's hurting anyone or that it's a problem, and he says he can stop whenever he wants. He justifies it by saying that she doesn't give herself to him enough, and that he does it so she won't have to. It's just an excuse," Ramiel shakes his head in disappointment as Emily's mom enters the room and begins to play with the girls.

"The things people say to convince themselves that they are without fault never cease to amaze me."

"I agree. I catch myself wondering what would happen if he could see what he truly was getting into and how it affected him, his wife, and daughter. If that would be enough to stop him or everyone else from sinning."

"You know it won't. It didn't work with past generations, and it won't work with these. They won't believe if they just see the signs and wonders. They have to believe what they are doing is wrong, not just see it. Look at what they consume now. Their 'monsters' aren't scary anymore but are celebrated. They produce and consume more and more stories on how evil is the new good guy, and is justified because of some other sin that happened to them and made them that way. When did two wrongs ever make one right?"

"Your exactly right. Death, sin, monsters don't have the same impact on them like it used to. The respect that humans once held for life and dignity for others and themselves is fading. Every day the world grows further away from the Master and His creation," Ramiel hangs his head in disappointment as he thinks on what his Emily may have to endure through her lifetime.

"Come on, let's cheer up. We have two amazing young ladies right here who still are young and haven't come to their time of choosing yet. Let's take advantage of this time we have together and do our job's so they can get all dolled up and play in peace," Sariel pokes his friend in the shoulder to remove the distraction of those monsters and sin and to return his attention to the reason that they are gathered tonight.

"You're absolutely right. Tonight is going to be great. We have these two amazing little ones with us, and we get to work together and not alone. It's going to be a fun night."

"That's it, my friend. I like this attitude."

The angels cheer up and resume their duties. For the next few hours, the ladies have an absolute blast as they sing, dance, apply makeup, play dress up, eat pizza, and laugh. The laughter of an innocent child is one of the sweetest things any creature could hear. Their joy motivates and encourages Sariel and Ramiel even more as minor skirmishes with the fallen happen through the night's activities. Hours pass and the time is now 9:30. All three girls are now curled up on the living-room couch watching the newest children's movie while Ralph sleeps in the master bedroom. The film is annoyingly interrupted as Becky's phone begins to vibrate without stopping until it receives her full attention.

"Give me a second, girls, something may have happened." She leans forward and grabs the device off the coffee table. "Oh man, I have to go. There's been a bad accident." She rises from her seat and turns toward the girls. "You two just stay here and finish the movie. In fact, you can start the next movie if I'm not back in time. Does that sound okay?" She asks as she pats their knees as if her allowance for a second movie will excuse her reason for the absence.

"Mom, what happened, why are you leaving?" Emily asks for fear of her mom's departure begins to consume her. "We're having so much fun. Don't ruin this, please. Please don't leave."

"Baby, I want to stay, I really do. But mommy has to help people that need her right now."

"But we need you right now," Emily lays the guilt on thick as she also reaches for her mother's hand.

"I get what you're saying, Emily, I really do. But there has been a big accident on the highway, and people are really hurt, and I must go help. They don't have enough people at the hospital right now to cover the ER. Do you understand? I'm not leaving because I want to, I'm going to help others."

"Fine, I understand." Emily sulks and manages to sink deeper into the cushion.

"Sara, are you going to be okay? Do you want to go home, or are you okay staying here for a bit while I'm gone? I will be back as soon as I can, but I can take you home if you want me to."

Sara looks to Emily for her reaction. She sees her friend's expression pleading her to stay, so she declines and says she will wait here and watch the movies.

"Great, okay. We are glad you're here. You girls be good."

Becky jumps up and bolts from the living room as she enters her bedroom and ignites the light. Ralph shouts some expletives as he is awakened by the intrusion of light and noise. She changes outfits and removes the pastel-colored makeup while explaining to her husband that she has been called in. She shouldn't be gone long, but she must go. Three fatalities have been confirmed as a nine-car pileup just happened on the highway.

Before exiting the room and eventually the house, she turns and tells her husband to stay awake and keep an eye out for the girls until she returns or until they fall asleep. Without waiting for a response, she jets out the door and is gone.

After she had told her husband to watch the girls, Ramiel and Sariel could hear a cackle of evil laughter escape the bedroom and make its way toward them in the living room. Ramiel is familiar with this sound as he has fought against it multiple times since the birth of Emily.

"Hey, did you hear that? Get ready, it's about to get heavy in here," Ramiel turns toward Sariel and activates his armor as he stands to attention with blades in hand and wings spread out. Sariel follows the action and gets ready for battle.

"What's about to happen? What can I expect?" Sariel asks as he scans the room, but primarily focuses on the master bedroom door.

"Lust, perversion, sexual immorality. These fallen are not your typical fallen. They are bigger than normal, and they are many. They have been the dad's welcome guests for a long time now."

As soon as Ramiel finishes his sentence, a thunderous shriek explodes from the master bedroom. Large black boney hands covered in disease and death grip the doorframe as they pull the remainder of their beings into sight. Nine large creatures of death make their way out of the room followed by their ensemble of minion-like fallen. Each of the nine demons stands over eight feet tall. They are draped in ragged hole-ridden clothes that resemble the darkest of shadows cast in the lowest of alleyways. Their limbs are long, frail, and jagged as they resemble the skeletons of their former selves as they follow Ralph to the nearest seat in the living room.

"They are ours tonight, Ramiel!" A voice bellows through the presence of the demonic as they make their way into the living room. "We have brought friends, in case you wanted to try and show out for your pathetic brother here. Tonight we are many. Now make this easy and step aside. Don't waste our time or yours for a lost cause. We have the father and mother. We will have the daughter, too."

The vile voice continues to spread across the fallen and speak as it spews tar and death-like curses at the two protectors through the enemies mouths. The liquid-like substance drips from their jaws as it is hurled toward the brothers of light. It dissolves and evaporates before making its intended target, as if an invisible barrier were protecting them.

"Through You, we will push down our enemies. Through Your name, we will trample those who rise up against us. For I will not trust in my bow, nor shall my sword save me. But You have saved us from our enemies, and have put to shame those who hated us. In God, we boast all day long, and praise Your name forever." As Ramiel finishes the scripture, he lunges forward like lightning and plants the blade in his right hand through the fallen's head that is standing directly behind and over Ralph. It penetrates all the way to the hilt of the sword. He turns the blade sideways and then sweeps it through the cheek of the creature, decapitating it, and swinging toward another.

The shock of what just happened quickly passes, and the other fallen, large and small, move toward the angels. Sariel also moves to attack as he swings both blades, creating a tornado of fire and destruction. Like a geyser, fallen spew out of the bedroom as Emily's dad comes into the living room and sits across the young ladies in his La-Z-Boy chair.

All around the living room and around the three humans, spirits fly and clash as battle rages. Swords are met by swords, wings slice through the decayed and weaker fallen, curses are spewed as the room is consumed with spiritual warfare. As Ramiel and Sariel fly back and forth through the room and through their enemies, they notice a few larger fallen bent over and now whispering into the ears of the father who is begrudgingly sitting there as he wishes he was still sleeping.

After a few moments, Ralph begins to rise from his seat with a devilish smirk on his face. He is looking at Sara lustfully as he is allowing her makeup and dress to tell his half-awake mind that she is older than presented. The two girls are oblivious to this as they continue to watch and sing along to the movie playing before them.

The battle is still raging, and the protectors are busy decimating their enemy in front of them. The fallen swarm with new members coming from the master bedroom using a coordinated attack to distract the two angels and impair their vision as Ralph and a handful of large fallen enter the kitchen.

"Hey, Sara, come here," he says as he comes to a stop and takes a seat at the breakfast-nook table. "Come on, come here. I want to see your pretty dress and makeup." He waves her over as she turned her attention to listen to his voice.

Sara looks back at her friend who is entrenched in the show, oblivious to her father's call. Sariel and Ramiel are distracted by the current combat formation and can't see what's taking place. The fallen have formed a thick wall covering any sight that may be beyond them. Sara doesn't want to leave her Emily, but remembers the words of her mother and obeys as she rises from her seat and heads his way. Vicious and vile cackling begin to be heard again from the kitchen area as the two angels continue to fight.

"What's going on? Who's laughing again?" Sariel asks as he slices through seven fallen with one swing of his blades. They are replaced with more of their kind as if the original never left, still obscuring the vision of the protectors.

"I don't know, I'll try to do a quick fly by and check out what's happening. They've just gotten really thick in here all of a sudden, and it's hard to move or see. Watch Emily for me."

As soon as Ramiel asked Sariel to watch Emily, he moved to check on the girls and noticed his Sara was no longer seated next to her friend. Before Ramiel could return with the devastating news, Sariel's intuition kicked in, and he knew precisely what was happening. Emily's dad is motioning for Sara to sit on his lap and tell him about her day. She is but three more steps away from him when Sariel roars, "No!"

As if Sara could hear him in the form of a whisper in her ear, she stops moving. Sariel explodes from his current combative situation and thrusts himself toward Sara and Ralph without thought of the wall of fallen or the danger around him. He begins spinning with his fiery blades straight ahead and his wings spread out as far as possible. Slicing through anything that they come into contact with. He has become a blender for the fallen, decimating his foes to grind and pulp.

He is flying forward like a missile of fire and absolute power as he continues the echo of his roar, "No!" He finds his target and thrusts his blades through the multiple large fallen that were whispering curses into the father's ear. They drop like ash from a tired and failing bonfire as he lands on the other side of the father's chair on one knee holding both blades out.

"No, that's okay, I'm just getting a drink for Emily. We can talk another time," Sara changes course and heads quickly toward the fridge and then back to her friend.

Sariel stands up and turns toward the remaining fallen that are battling Ramiel. "Out, in the name of the Master!" Each fallen, having seen and heard what just happened, quiver as they retreat back toward the bedroom.

Both Ramiel and Sariel focus on the father as he rises from the chair. Disgust and shame gallop through him as the thought of what he was trying to do sweeps over him like air escaping into space. The voices of vile intentions are replaced with the eerie quiet of heinous embarrassment and scandalous recollection of what he was just doing. His spirit emerges from his corpse and takes a long gasp of air as if it had been drowning for some time. It appears weak and old, as if in the late stages of an aggressive cancer. It sinks back inside his cavity as the father rises from his chair and lowers his head.

"Listen, I'm exhausted. It's been a long day, so I'm gonna go lie down. Knock if you need anything. I'll be awake."

The distance from the kitchen to his room door is short, but the journey is long as he tries to hide his face of reprehensible guilt for the monster he almost became. His corpse is greeted again and swallowed by old friends as they consume his spirit once more after he enters his room.

Moments after his bedroom door shuts, the front door opens, and Becky comes inside. She tells the girls that she was sent the wrong text and they had more than enough staff to cover the situation. All three ladies return to watching and cuddling as if nothing ever happened. As for Ramiel, he is in shock as he has never witnessed a protector do anything like what Sariel just did.

"How did you do that? How did she hear you?" He asks as he lifts his mouth from the floor in astonishment.

"I don't know. Haven't you done that before? Hasn't he ever tried something like that with Emily?"

"No, tonight was a first. He only does those things with himself or his wife, but he's never tried to touch her," Ramiel pauses for a moment before continuing to speak, "I didn't know we could talk to them or that they could even hear us."

"Yeah, I don't know how that happened. I didn't know we could do that either. It just came over me, and I screamed it out. As if the Master was speaking through me."

Chapter 9

Three months, seven days, and nine hours since Ralph wanted and tried to molest Sara. Three months of torture, confusion, and guilt. He never thought that would happen. He never imagined that his condition was like that. He blames exhaustion, her makeup, and fake façade of maturity, as well as the late hour. He blames everything he can until one day he runs out of options and blames himself. He doesn't dare tell or admit anything to anyone. Nothing happened physically; he didn't touch her—but he did. In his mind, he completed despicable acts: acts of immorality and disgust, acts of lust and death.

Ramiel watches on as the fallen's attention recently has been on consuming Ralph, allowing him to have a minor break from their full attention and attacks.

The morning sun rises for the third month and eighth day since that awful night, but something is different about this day. Becky is not home yet because of work, which is normal, but Ralph should be entering Emily's room to wake her and prepare her for school. Ramiel is cautiously optimistic as he wonders if her father merely has allowed her to sleep in. The peace that Emily has while sleeping is as a breeze of air floating across fields of wheat and nature. Carrying petals and scents of just moments before. He takes a few steps toward their door to listen and examine if the lights are on in her parent's room or if something is happening.

Ramiel begins to grow paranoid and cautious as he continues his journey and steps toward her parent's door. It's too eerily quiet. Shadows of fallen are seen skimming from under the doorframe, yet they are miraculously quiet. Not knowing what to expect but fallen and loss, he readies his equipment and mind to prepare for anything. He phases through the closed door and enters the parent's domain.

Immediate, anxiety and panic rise in him like a geyser preparing to erupt. Fallen quickly grab hold of Ramiel on all four limbs. Momentarily, he is stuck in place as he witnesses the scene laid out before him like a brutal car accident. Emily's father is lying on his bed with a gun in one hand and a bottle in the other. He is not known for being a drunk, but the whispers of two large fallen angels of death have been speaking to him for what looks like the entire evening.

There is still hope as he hasn't pulled the trigger. Ramiel snaps out of awe and breaks into action. He twists his hips in a rapid clockwise direction, forcing his core and wings to follow, causing them to cut and free the enemies grasp. While doing this, Ramiel glances back at Emily's door to see that she is still asleep. He takes both blades and begins to fight off fallen that have flooded the room to watch the spectacle of suicide.

As if the father were a defeated gladiator in the arena, the fallen have cast their judgment and have condemned him to death. Ramiel is not fighting for Ralph, who still has a chance and who is still loved by the Master. No, Ramiel is fighting for Emily so that she won't have to wake and see what is going to happen.

The fight continues, but no progress has been made as the enemy has a stronghold in this room. Ramiel is stuck near the entrance as the waves of fallen gush from Ralph's chest and stop him from advancing. Flashes of light and noise of thunder fill the room as the two sides wage war.

Suddenly and without warning, Ralph sits up in bed and turns to get on his knees as he starts sobbing uncontrollably and points the tip of his weapon directly into his mouth. The sobs and noise can be heard throughout the home, and Emily begins to toss and turn as her peaceful dreams start to fade, and her body moves around as if to wake. Ramiel senses this and cries out with a loud voice, "No!" as he thrusts himself toward the trigger of the gun, following the example that Sariel had done. He rams both blades into the firing pin as if to jam the weapon and stop it from completing its duty.

The fallen take advantage of Ramiel's situation and begin to swing, tear, and rip parts of his armor and flesh away. His wings dance back and forth, trying to stop as much as they can, but they aren't able to stop the entire bombardment from the fallen. He continues to shout in defiance against Ralph's actions. He begins to slowly pull the trigger as two large fallen whisper death, false peace, and misery in his ears—offering an eternal escape and exit from his present nightmare if he just were to pull the trigger. More and more blows fall all over Ramiel, but he continues to hold his grip and blades in place. Praying and asking the Master to let this work, Ramiel is mortified to move or change tactics. The pain is a small and grateful price to pay to protect Emily.

He squeezes the trigger, and the gun doesn't fire. As if it were jammed, the hammer won't fall. He intensifies his grip and chokes the trigger, like a snake preparing its meal. However, the outcome is the same—the gun won't fire. Ramiel is elated to see his plan is working. He doesn't know how long he can hold it, but he won't allow himself to move while the barrel is still in Ralph's mouth.

"Daddy?" Emily rubs her eyes pushing aside any residual sleep and hoping to get a better look at what her father is doing. "Daddy what are you doing?"

Panic reigns over Ralph at the sight of his little one. Immediately he drops the weapon and addresses Emily.

"Nothing, sweetie. I'm just cleaning my gun and giving it a polish. You know, like when you breathe on a window or glasses to wipe stuff off. Everything is fine, baby. Just give me a minute and close the door."

As she follows his command, he not only collapses physically but spiritually and emotionally. Every emotion he was just feeling, begin to pour out of him. The fallen immediately vanish and Ramiel loses his grip as the gun falls into the sea of blankets. Ralph sinks his head into the closest pillow and begins to scream. No words, yet he is speaking. Anguish, humiliation, pain, and sorrow are all being sung from his solo into the pillow. Ramiel whispers a prayer as he leaves the room, causing his body to heal upon his exit.

Emily makes her way into the kitchen and prepares a bowl of cereal. She knows something else was going on, but she is too frightened of him to explore or ask about it. She loves him regardless of the fear she has of him. She believes that he will come out of there eventually, but in the meantime, she should eat something and continue to wake. She pours milk over the cereal and takes a seat at the very spot her dad sat just a few months ago.

In between slurps and crunching, she hears faint cries coming from her parents' bedroom. Ramiel stands guard, ready for another fight, but no one comes as the invitation was not delivered. He mourns for Ralph and what he's going through, but Ramiel's primary focus of sadness is on Emily as she is so young to have to contend with such thoughts and fear.

Ralph wipes away tears and tries to compose himself before leaving his bed. Something powerful happened at that moment his daughter opened the door. Not only did she stop him from pulling the trigger, but she also pulled away a veil from over his eyes. As if he were genuinely able to see himself and what his actions were about to do, remorse and self-examination take over. The man he saw through his daughter's eyes pierced harder than any angelic blade ever could. It caused all inhabitants to immediately vacate the premises. He saw love. Her simple presence reminded him that she was worth getting better for, and that regardless of any fear she may have or shame he has, he does love her. Her presence was the sobering cold shower his spirit needed to wake from his self-loathing and activity of ultimate regret.

"I'm so sorry. I'm sorry, I'm sorry, I'm sorry. I never meant for that to happen. I never meant for any of this to happen. I'm sorry," He whispers to himself as he slowly makes his way off of the bed and toward the kitchen.

Over the next few weeks, Emily and Becky notice a tone change coming from the man of the house. He is more patient and tries to spend time with the girls rather than merely retreating to his room after a long day. He tries to be present more and even plays a few times with his daughter, but more importantly—and sadly—he attempts to fix himself all alone. He doesn't ask the Master for help, so the fallen eventually return to the empty residence, reclaiming the territory. The new fallen are more prominent than before, but they battle not only Ramiel but the thought of what he almost did. His self-pity and therapy buy the protector some additional time before he turns back to lust and perversion, making the past situation even worse.

As the following weeks pass, the father has now become more involved with his family, even attending a couple of Sunday services with them. The church, in fact, announced that it would be attending a large conference held at the city arena. A larger-than-life evangelist will be coming into town next Saturday to offer guidance and support to all that attend. Sara and her family said they would participate, as well as most of the congregation and the big five. This causes Emily to want to go, and eventually her parent's request off from work to attend as well. Ralph said yes to going, not genuinely hearing what was really asked of him.

Before they know it, the big day arrives. Both families find spaces in a parking garage that's only three blocks away. As the families march together toward the arena, amazement consumes them as they are in awe of the spectacle of lights and loud music. It appears to be more of a concert than a church service, and the number of people that are attending is staggering. Ramiel and Sariel are also in shock at the amount of light and darkness clashing along the streets and at the entrance to the event. A larger-than-life banner hangs over the arena's gateway: "Come and Witness God's Love with World-Famous Evangelist Michael Jubilee."

Chapter 10

The pastor of their church reserved seating for his congregation on the main floor toward the back of the seating section. Majority of the elderly with the group are very thankful for the location as the closest bathroom is less than twenty yards away. The big five are in attendance, as well as seven other followers and forty-two knowers, including both Sara and Emily's families. All of the protectors and warriors form a wall around the group with the big five making up the actual circle and the other angels filling in gaps.

The arena is massive as its maximum capacity is 22,500. All seats on all levels that are in front of the stage will be filled. Even seats behind the stage are being filled with onlookers as monitors are raised that they may also partake in the festivities. The arena is only a few hundred shy of meeting its maximum occupancy mark. The stage is outlined with lights, monitors, musical instruments, and speakers. It's decorated with large rugs covering its floor, and the banner hanging behind the center platform is almost an exact copy of the one outside. The only difference being that Michael Jubilee's name is bold and italic and more massive than the rest of the wording.

In the spiritual realm, the arena resembles that of a clear midnight sky. Darkness is the backdrop as it's littered with large and small pockets of light. The fallen's presence easily take command of the arena as it fills.

Still, the visibility of angels is apparent as they shine like the sun off of the waves of the black ocean. Each group and each individual angel is close enough to another so that they aren't truly alone. Sariel and Ramiel's group is large enough that they may be able to handle their own congregation, but they aren't quite sure at the moment how well they will be able to assist others. Even with the big five, the numbers and size of the collected fallen are a force to be reckoned with. Nine other groups resemble the number of angels like that of the young girls' congregation. However, no other group has the actual physical size that Ramiel and Sariel have due to their big friends, but they still have the numbers.

This scenario is different than the school-coordinated attacks that they have grown used to. Outside of those small souls needing protectors, everyone else is here by choice and free will. There are no coordinating messenger angels to help guide and strategize a victory, and there are no warrior angels here outside of the entourage of followers. This event is a celestial skirmish of massive proportions.

The arena now fills to its brim, so the music starts. The crowd is guided by the words on the jumbotron and screens throughout the stadium. The stage is filled with talented people of all race, size, and age. Beautiful is such a small word to describe the praise they are singing. The band moves and reacts like one. Their voices and instruments are one as they continue with their coordinated set of empty faith and self-promotion.

The fallen begin to sway back and forth in perfect unison. They don't lift a single decayed finger during the music. They just swing left to right, left to right, following their own tune and motion, creating a wave of death and distraction. The protectors and warrior angels grow nervous at the patience of the fallen. The groups have formed, and their armor is on display, but the angels are mesmerized by their opponent's unity and coordination.

Every few seconds, an angel would swipe into the dark mass of death, striking multiple foes. For each fallen slain, two more take their place as if they were a hydra. This continues throughout the praise and worship service. As soon as the songs are over and the musicians leave the stage, the audience takes a seat, and the fallen stop in place and begin to hiss and laugh at the angels. They do this while the lead pastor of the city's largest church introduces the guest speaker.

"Hello, hello, everybody. How are we doing today?"

The audience erupts with shouts of praise and greetings.

"That's fantastic. My name is Pastor Jacobs, and I have the absolute honor of introducing a wonderful and humble man of God to you today. This man has traveled the world, circling the globe six times so far with his ministry, speaking to millions of people about our wonderful savior."

The crowd erupts again with applause.

"Hundreds of thousands have accepted the Lord at his conferences and meetings. He has spoken with world leaders from fifty-two nations. He has written four New York Times bestselling books. He and his wife recently had a cameo in the newest Christian drama, 'Why God, why me?'

"In addition to all of this, he still finds the time to chat with his followers online and continues to post those ridiculously funny videos on YouTube. His most-watched video to date has over eleven million views. That's not that bad," Jacobs turns to his right as he looks backstage in the direction of the one he is referring to. He laughs, turns his attention back to the crowd and continues, "Everyone, please stand to your feet once again and help me introduce Michael Jubilee!"

The crowd follows orders and erupts with admiration and praise as the man takes the stage, hugs his fake acquaintance, and thanks him for his kind words.

While this is happening, the fallen have yet to advance forward. They continue to stand still, hiss, and crackle at the angels, as if holding a secret that they will never tell. Ramiel and Sariel's congregation jumps to their feet—all of them—as Michael takes the stage. Everyone is so elated to hear from this prestigious man. The arena continues to applaud when all of a sudden, the angels feel and hear a loud crash. *Crash, slam, smack,* and *thud.* The noise grows louder and louder as Michael motions for the crowd to calm and sit so he can begin to speak. The bombardment of noise climbs behind the stage and comes to a halt as Michael is finally able to get the crowd to take their seats.

"Well hello, everyone. My name is Michael Jubilee."

A *roar* rips and screams through the arena as the last syllable leaves Michael's mouth. The sound is chaotic and monstrous as it could only be produced by a fallen dragon.

The beast explodes onto the stage behind his puppet, taking his position of marionettist. This creature is the size of a mountain. It stands over fifty feet tall while its wingspan is over eighty feet wide. Its head is the size of a large moving truck, and its opened roaring mouth produces white and blue flames, hot enough to contest any metal on earth. Its front teeth resemble spears as they are long, sharp, and drenched with decay. The horns coming off of its head are spiraled like a long secret stairwell that ends in sword-like sharpness.

Death drips from the sides of its mouth as it now motions its head back and forth. Its arms and legs are like trees as they are stable and robust and swing back and forth with what looks like little to no effort. Its tail continues beyond its core unit for an additional twenty feet. It's covered in spikes and scales as it appears to move like its own individual entity. The entirety of the beast is colored in midnight black with hints of fire that erupt and protrude from open pores.

This being does not look small or frail compared to the fallen in the arena. This creature is full and substantial as it stands for death and destruction. Upon the dragon and Michael's introduction, the fallen in the crowd completely stop all action and stand quietly in place, as if a solitaire program that is waiting for its next command.

"Ain't God good? I've been blessed over the years, and I want to talk to you all tonight about my blessings and how you can unlock those for yourselves. Are you ready?"

"Amen!" the crowd shouts with joy.

"Wow, I love when God's people talk back."

"Woohoo!" the arena erupts again as it's prompted, too, by his flattery.

"Well, praise God, this is going to be a great time together. Everyone turn with me if you will to—"

The big five immediately begin to quote scripture as they prepare for the onslaught. The rest of the angels quickly join with them in their prayer as they all feel the heat of hell rising from the floor. At any moment the facility is going to explode with violence.

"The Lord is my shepherd; I shall not want. He maketh me to lie down in green pastures: he leadeth me beside the still waters. He restoreth my soul: he leadeth me in the paths of righteousness for his name's sake. Yea, though I walk through the valley of the shadow of death, I will fear no evil: for thou art with me; thy rod and thy staff they comfort me. Thou preparest a table before me in the presence of mine enemies: thou anointest my head with oil; my cup runneth over. Surely goodness and mercy shall follow me all the days of my life: and I will dwell in the house of the Lord for ever."

They finish with a righteous yell as they all lift their right arms into the air. Together, they bring them back down hard and fast as they pierce the earth beneath them, causing a shockwave, knocking back the first several rows of fallen down.

The angels move to the offensive after the fallen hit the ground. The ones in groups move in and out of each other like pistons rising and falling in a car engine. After a strike and deadly blow, the lead angel retreats to the back of the group to only go again in a few short moments. They repeat this action over and over again. This causes an endless wave of light and destruction to the fallen that are on the ground.

The angels that are not in a group, but nearby, step as close as they can to their comrades, hoping to benefit from them. They swing wildly and furiously, striking a blow on every flick of the wrist. Still, they are vulnerable as the fallen take advantage of their situation. Like an outnumbered lion, the fallen act like hyenas and circle their prey. Slowly picking and prodding, they manage to get through the lone angelic defense of the protectors not in groups.

As the fallen pick away at the armor and eventual flesh of the angel, opportunities arise, and they don't miss their mark. The dragon on stage sees what is happening and points to each lone protector when the time is ripe. As his command is followed, a wave of fallen rise and sweep over the protectors. They are held down and made to watch as the fallen whisper into the ears of the young ones.

"God is good. You are good. Just say you're sorry, and all will be forgiven. Just say you're sorry, and then play your games on your phone. Don't worry about this adult stuff. God loves you and won't let anything happen to you. Just be who you are. You can't change that. Your parents will be so proud of you if they see you pray. They will probably get you a gift if you do it. Just do it, and you will be fine."

The heartbroken protectors watch as their young ones are influenced into believing a lie throughout the service. They cry out as they see the moment of choosing happen before them. Beams of light shoot down and through their skulls as knowledge descends on them like a plane on a runway. It enters their minds, excusing the shroud of innocence as it is lifted and replaced with the new tenant.

This is the moment in time for their first opportunity to choose the Master for themselves or not. The innocent decide to get the attention of their parents during the preaching and to move on from the ramblings of the evangelic false teacher.

Tears fall from the trapped protectors' eyes as one by one, their protected become knowers. After the choice is made, the angel is excused from their duty and must leave as its service is not currently required. This process happens at least seventy-four times while the speaker is preaching. The lone protectors that are near a more significant number of angels benefit from their brothers and aren't pinned down so quickly.

The service and battle rages for over an hour as the numbers of angels continue to diminish, and darkness continues to grow. Finally, as the evangelist is wrapping up, the dragon stands as high as he can and commands all fallen to stop and regroup. They retract themselves into tight cylinders of death, at least twenty feet away from their closest enemy.

"And that's when my dog came home, and I knew God was real. You see, it's the small things at first, almost like a test, to see if we can handle it. God won't just give everyone a Mercedes like the one I have outside. He didn't give me one at first. My dad did."

The crowd ignites with laughter.

"You have to be willing to start somewhere and work for it. You have to tithe, you have to read the books, like my book *Growing and Prospering: Shifting Into the Gear and Speed That God Wants for You.* You have to tell everyone about Him, and you have to pray.

"Speaking of prayer, I would like us all to bow our heads at this moment. I want us all to be honest with ourselves. To acknowledge where we truly are with Him. If you don't know where you are with him, or if you've screwed up and maybe burnt the clutch a little too much lately. With all heads bowed and eyes closed, I want you to raise your hand."

As the audience reacts to his emotional and empty story, they willingly follow his command as they self-reflect to his mirror of God. Hundreds and thousands of hands rise into the air, claiming they need the Master. Michael moves fast, back and forth, across the stage shouting how good it is to see God moving and people recognizing the move. He yells and claps as he points and acknowledges each hand that he sees.

"There's another one, and another, and another. God is truly moving now. There's another one there and there, and another and another. People, you are doing great. Continue to open your heart and obey the Lord. In a second, I want all those in attendance that raised their hand to repeat after me. You can whisper it, shout it, mime it, or simply speak it. God knows your heart and where you're at. Just repeat after me, okay?"

The dragon lets out a thunderous roar, one that could be compared to the roar of a hurricane. It stretches out both arms in command for a full frontal attack. The fallen begin to rise as their mass grows into instruments of death and destruction. Thousands of fallen combine, creating wrecking balls that are headed straight toward the larger groups of angels. They make impact and shatter against their foe as the evangelist begins his deceitful prayer.

"Repeat after me. Dear God, I am a sinner. I will always be a sinner. I need you. By your mercy and grace, I can be more, and I can be covered by your blood. You said that your blood covers a multitude of sins. Please cover mine now. Please forgive me and come into my heart that I may be with you forever. That you accept me as I am and who I am. But that you will also help prepare me for the gear that you want me to be in. Help me to shift and to grow into your other gears as well. Help me, God, as I say this prayer and become yours forever. In the Holy Father's name, I pray. Amen."

Wave after wave after wave crash against Ramiel, Sariel, and the rest of their congregation. A few fallen make it through their ranks, but the ones that do are quickly smitten by a few of the group's warrior angels. The big five are in full effect as they fight and scurry like every other angel. The difference being that their impact parts the fallen like the Red Sea compared to their brothers. Slicing and swinging, the group manages to hold off the hordes of fallen. Their victory is hard-fought and overall spoiled as the fallen were able to affect so many in attendance. After the prayer was complete, an additional 237 protected became knowers, all for the attention of loved ones or to believe and cling on to the lies of the enemy. Hope is not lost for them, but the road is not easy.

Michael Jubilee finishes and exits the stage followed by his dragon. Pastor Jacobs thanks all those in attendance, credits Michael Jubilee for helping over 4,500 dedicate their lives or renew their vows to Christ, reminds every one of the gift shops set up in the hallways, and then dismisses the crowd.

"Wow, what good points. I never thought of it like that before. Did any of you?" Bill asks, pointing to his wife and Emily's parents.

"Yeah, it was a good lesson. So good in fact that now I'm hungry. You guys want to all go grab dinner together?" Becky asks the group as they stand and wait for the aisle to thin out before leaving their row.

"Yeah, sure, that sounds great. What do you all want?" Nancy replies as she looks to Bill for support and approval.

"Yeah, that does sound good. We will go wherever you want to."

"Babe, any thoughts?" Becky asks Ralph.

"Umm, sure. What if we went to that burger spot by the house? Every restaurant near here is about to get slammed. Plus, they have those amazing shakes. The girls will love them."

"Oh, yes please, can I have a milkshake?" Emily begins to jump in place at the sound of having a milkshake.

"Me, too. Please, pretty please," Sara joins her friend in enthusiasm.

The girls beg and plead, and the moms finally agree. The families also concur for Bill and Nancy to go ahead of them and try to grab a table for the group as the two girls want to ride back together.

Eventually, they are able to exit the arena and arrive at their cars. One vehicle takes off and heads for the destination, and the other continues to load the little ladies. While all this is happening, Sariel and Ramiel are silent. They don't nod to each other; they don't look for other angels; they merely follow their little ones. They have never witnessed a time of choosing like that before. Their first experience of the evangelistic event is shrouded in loss as they primarily observed the protected become knowers.

They also have never seen a dragon that close before. To see how it unified the fallen and was able to influence so many protected into becoming knowers is a very surreal and humbling experience.

All members eventually enter the vehicle, buckle in, and head toward dinner. The two little ones are on their devices as the parents navigate the quickest exit of downtown. Ralph makes an immediate sharp right turn to beat a light from turning red. In doing so, Sara loses grip of her device and it slips to the ground.

"Um, can someone please help me? I dropped my tablet, and I can't reach it since I'm buckled in."

"You need to be careful and slow down while you drive. It's not a race. They are getting a table for all of us. Hold on a second honey, and I'll get it for you." Becky grumbles as she unbuckles, hits her husband's arm, and turns to grab the device that is now hidden under the second row of seating.

"Why'd you hit me? I didn't mean for that to happen. I just didn't want to have to wait for all those cars for a simple right-hand turn. I'm driving, and you need to—"

His explanation and rant are interrupted by the impact of a speeding SUV that ferociously invades their four-door sedan starting on the driver's side.

Chapter 11

"No!" Ramiel screams less than a second before the two vehicles collide.

The reckless missile of death impacts with Emily's parent's vehicle on the driver's side with a charging force close to sixty miles per hour. The family car was positioned in the left-hand lane of a one-way street in the downtown metro area. Emily and Ralph are seated on that side while Sara and Becky are on the other side. The car rapidly folds into itself as it is invaded by the unwelcome guest of a large SUV. Glass shatters and breaks instantaneously as it floats through the air, waiting to find a new home to land on.

The impact of the SUV causes the car to flip sideways several times like a wave making its way to shore. While airborne, the vehicle collides with a tree that decorated the city sidewalk, causing the vehicle to rotate 180 degrees. What once was a full-sized four-door sedan is now smaller than a compact car. The driver's side has completely collapsed in on itself as metal is woven with metal and flesh. The vehicle finally lands, flipped on its top, and now facing in the opposite direction than what it was initially traveling.

Becky was violently tossed around the interior of the vehicle, making contact with multiple points of debris, Sara's body, and destruction before exiting the vehicle's front window on the third rotation. Her body is broken and lifeless as it lands and skies across the pavement like skates to frozen ice. Emily and her dad are swallowed whole as the casing of the vehicle engulfs them and wraps them in an unwanted cocoon of metal and debris.

Sara is still strapped to her seat, causing her body to not be allowed to escape the newly formed minefield of death and destruction. Her head hits multiple points inside of the vehicle as it swings back and forth in her seat. Both of Sara's arms snap and break as well as her left leg as Becky's body makes impact with Sara's multiple times before physics commands Becky to make her exit from the vehicle. Sara is knocked unconscious before the sedan makes its final stop.

Ramiel and Sariel turn and move with the vehicle unencumbered by the physical transformation that has taken place. Their beings are dragged along merely because of their connection with the two girls. The car comes to its stop, and both angels stand upright and are now positioned on top of the bottom of the sedan. They look around to get a quick bearing of what just happened. Vehicles, knowers, followers, angels, and fallen all come to a halt as they witness the collision. The fallen laugh uncontrollably as they look and point at the protectors.

The humans and vehicles come to screeching stops as they just stand and stare before reacting. Angels weep and begin to pray as they see death inside and out of the family transportation as Ralph and Becky have already succumbed to their wounds.

The vehicle that made an impact with them skids to a stop only a few meters away from the collision. The vehicle's front bumper and motor absorb most of its damage after the crash, causing its front airbags to be deployed. A bruised young and slightly cut teenager begins to feel the top of her head as blood runs down her cheek. Her hand finds the trail of blood as she moves her fingers into sight to examine the damp substance.

"I'm not drunk. I didn't even drink that much. I'm not drunk. I was texting a friend. That's it. Yeah, that's it. It was just a quick text, just a quick text. It was just a text. Where's my phone? It was just a text." She tells herself as she slurs her speech, trying to come to reason with what just happened.

The teenager begins to cry as she repeats herself over and over, suffering from the shock of the accident and the sight of her own blood on her fingers. Then the young girl quickly transforms from crying to complete heartache and remorse as she fixates on the lifeless body of Emily's mom lying in front of her vehicle about twenty yards away.

This entire incident has taken less than five seconds, but to all those involved, it has felt like a millennium. Fallen grab the souls of both parents and race them to heaven for both judgment and to claim their prize. Additional fallen begin to crowd the vehicle as they eagerly wait and thirst for the two young souls. The nearby angels leave their posts and begin to wage war on behalf of Ramiel and Sariel, giving them time to react to everything that is happening.

Ramiel jumps down from his current position to check on Emily; what he finds almost takes his breath away. Physically, he can't see the entirety of Emily's body as she is wrapped in the dress of the vehicle; only her left arm and hand present themselves. Spiritually, he watches as her heart beats slower and slower, and her bright spirit begins to fade.

Sariel also jumps from atop the vehicle and lands on Sara's side. She is still strapped in her seat, hanging upside down. Her limbs hang like meat on hooks as she appears to be lifeless. The crowd hasn't reached her side of the vehicle yet as her door is now positioned on the opposite side of the road's sidewalk and facing a metallic and glass building. Sariel begins to assess the damage to Sara, while Ramiel drops and prays. He worships and prays as that is all he can do, knowing the state that Emily is currently in.

"And, behold, there came a great wind from the wilderness, and smote the four corners of the house, and it fell upon the young men, and they are dead; and I only am escaped alone to tell thee. Then Job arose, and rent his mantle, and shaved his head, and fell down upon the ground, and worshipped, and said, Naked came I out of my mother's womb, and naked shall I return thither: the LORD gave, and the LORD hath taken away; blessed be the name of the LORD." Repeatedly, Ramiel says those words as he begins to fall into himself, rocking back and forth as he watches her light continue to fade.

Sariel shouts and screams as he begins to tear at the seatbelt holding Sara into place. "I can do all this through him who gives me strength."

It's not often an angel can or will interact with the human world, but Sariel takes advantage that no one can see Sara's side of the vehicle. He's not going to allow his precious little one to hang there and suffer or die. The car's engine ignites with flames, pushing Sariel to act even faster.

"I can do all this through him who gives me strength!" he shouts one last time as the seatbelts give way and her body falls limp, crashing to the ground of broken metal and glass.

Upon her landing like a lifeless doll, Sariel grabs her under her armpits and drags her away from the car to the edge of the neighboring goliath of a building. Still, no one is able to see what is happening as her body is blocked by metal, plastic, and destruction. As Sara is being dragged away, she opens her eyes, and for a split second, she believes she sees Sariel's angelic face. Not knowing who that is or what is going on, she panics and passes back out, overwhelmed by the pain racing through her body.

"Sara, please, please, please, Sara, please," Sariel begins to weep and plead over her as he wipes her face and kisses her forehead. "Please, Sara, come on. Wake up. Master, please do something!" Sariel screams as he looks toward home. "Master, please do something!"

Fallen are now gathering around him, cackling and laughing as they see her body grow weaker with every passing moment. They don't attack; they just wait like vultures for the lifeless body to breathe its last breath. The cackling and snarling are interrupted and stopped by the swipe of a blade as another angel comes to stand guard to allow his brother time. Sariel looks at his brother with tears in his eyes and just begins to weep over little Sara.

"There's another one over here. Come on!" a police officer shouts as he notices Sara's leg on the other side of destruction and fire. Unintentionally, he interrupts the spiritual moment running toward and landing right beside little Sara. He begins CPR to try and keep her alive. Her pulse is feeble, but she is still here. She is alive, but only barely.

Another millennium passes as the ambulance pulls up. They quickly load Sara on a gurney and rush her to the closest hospital. Sariel climbs on top of the vehicle as it speeds off with its sirens blaring as loud as possible.

Ramiel watches his friend exit the scene as he sits next to the broken vehicle that is encasing his little Emily's body. Even though she is physically trapped inside the car, he can see past the twisted metal. His hand is unencumbered as he reaches for Emily's hand to hold. Every second that passes her life force fades, and she grows weaker. He tries talking to her as he can't do anything else.

"Come on, baby, you're going to be fine. I won't let anything happen to you. I promised I would protect you. Come on, Emily, just hold on. They're coming to get you out. I love you. I love you so much. Master, please tell them to hurry. Please make a way. Please keep her here. Let me fulfill my duty as protector until her time of choosing. Please don't let her go. Not yet. She's not ready. Please, not yet." Ramiel begins to panic as he can see the life drain even faster from Emily's being.

In similar fashion to what happened with Sariel, the fallen creep around Ramiel and wait for death to arrive. They know where she is headed; they know where her parents are now. Two warrior angels appear and interrupt their flaunting as they smite the surrounding fallen, creating a plain of quiet space for Ramiel. He continues to mourn as he sits there and holds her lifeless hand. He can't do anything else, and the feeling makes him feel weak and scared. For a moment, he almost feels human.

"I love you so much. I swear, I love you so much. You are the greatest gift that could have ever been given to me. I'm so sorry I let you down. I'm sorry I didn't stop the car. I'm so sorry, my love." He slowly turns his head toward Emily's chest as he hears her last breath travel and escape through her body.

"I love you so much. I'm so sorry, baby girl. I'm so sorry," he drops his head and sorrowfully weeps while holding on to her lifeless hand until he can't anymore.

The warrior angels are dismissed as she passes from this world and the fallen move in. They cackle and climb over Ramiel's frozen body. They reach their destination and turn back to mock her protector, "Good job. You sure did a bang-up job watching over her, didn't you? Don't worry. We will take care of her for now, son of the Master."

Her soul emerges from its carriage and looks toward its protector. A faint and tired smile is on display as they make eye contact.

Ramiel reaches to stroke her spirit's cheek. As his hand moves toward its destination, the fallen grab her soul from her corpse and blasts off into the celestial space like rockets headed to a faraway moon.

Ramiel begins to sob and sob. He is broken; he is hurt; he feels love and loss. He rises and readies his gear. In a righteous rage, he begins to swing wildly and free, like a fish flopping out of water. He repeatedly finds his mark as fallen crumble all around him in every direction. He screams and weeps with each swing. He continues this dance of misery and pain until he finds himself in the arms of the Master.

Chapter 12

Ramiel is no longer dressed as a protector as he finds himself sobbing in the arms of the Master. He is no longer on that city street but in flight, traveling through the cosmos, heading home. He looks up, not moving his head and realizes where he is and begins to cry even more. The realization that he is on his way back home only further solidifies that Emily is gone. As if tears were limitless for angels, Ramiel tries to use everything at his disposal. In between breaths and moans, he hears additional cries and sobbing. He lifts his head away for a moment from the Master's shoulder to see what is happening. He sees the Master sobbing as well with His head lowered as He too expresses the pain of this loss.

"Master, why are you crying?" Ramiel asks as he tries to compose himself to speak.

"I loved her so much. I loved them so much. I love them, and I miss them, Ramiel. I truly miss them, and I want them back," the Master continues to sob as He answers the question. "They were so special, and I loved them so much. I can't accept that they're gone. It hurts. The pain hurts, just like it did on that day so long ago."

"Master, I don't understand," Ramiel begins to collect and sober himself as the gesture of the Master's tears is too much for him to handle.

"I had known them since before I created you, Ramiel. I've known Emily for a very long time. I know everything there is to know about her. I know her complete construction physically and her personality. I knew she had a weird love for frogs before she did."

"She did obsess with frogs and her stuffed toy frog for a very long time," Ramiel chuckles mid-sob as he recalls Emily as a toddler dragging her favorite toy around everywhere.

"I knew she didn't like grape jelly, but only strawberry jelly. I knew she loved to dance before her first breath. I knew everything."

"Then why? If you knew everything, then why did it happen? Why didn't she choose you and why isn't she here now? Why not? Please help me understand."

"It's not that simple, Ramiel. You know this. It's not an easy answer or question."

"Tell me. I deserve to know. I need to know. Why then did you let this happen?" Ramiel separates himself from the embrace of the Master as he glides a few feet back to hear His response.

"Ramiel, now is not the time. Now is the time for grief and remembrance, not answers or some type of justification," the Master hangs His head as he continues to mourn.

"Please, sir. Please tell me. Help me to understand. Help me to see what You see."

The Master shakes his head as it slowly rises from its downward position. "Okay, fine, Ramiel. I will try and explain it to you."

Ramiel stands at the ready as he waits for the answer and justification of what just happened.

"It happened because I love them."

"What?" Ramiel is shocked by the answer, yet never shows disrespect with his response or attitude.

"Ramiel, I love them so much that I will let them choose life or death. They get to choose whether they want heaven or hell. I didn't do this or force it on them. They choose this, not Me. It kills Me that they made this choice, but I allow them to do it because I love them."

"You let them choose? I don't understand. There is a process of the choosing scenario. It is sacred and law. It's not a car accident. Why would You give them so much power? Why do You let them choose death?"

"I know the process. I set it into motion long before I created their earth. Let me ask you a question, Ramiel. Why do you love me?" The Master sobers up His heartache as He begins to ask His question.

"I love you because you are the Master. You are Lord of all. You are the Creator, the great I Am."

"Yes, I am those things, but why do you love me?"

"I don't understand. What other reason is there that I love you? I just do. I just love you and will always love you."

"Exactly. You always will. I created you to love Me. You didn't have a say or choice in the matter. You and your brothers were created to obey and to love Me. Your brothers that fell didn't stop loving me until they were cast out. They just believed another was my equal, but they still loved me until I removed that love and life from them. You love me because I say it's so and it is so. They don't have that construct. They have free will. They can love or hate me. It's their choice."

"Yes, but why not remove that from them?"

"Because that's not true love. True love is allowing another to wholeheartedly love you back, or allowing that person to walk away.

"I love you, Ramiel, but your love for Me in return is there because I put it there. You will always love Me, and I treasure you for it. That's why I gave you charge to watch over little Emily because you love Me so. And you did a beautiful job with her. You truly did. But this remorse you're experiencing, this sadness and sense of loss that you are going through, is what I am talking about. It's love."

"I don't understand. How is this love? How is love such pain."

"True love is when another accepts you for who you are and still loves you. True love is allowing that being the choice to love you back. I made you and your brothers to love and to obey Me.

"One of your brothers got so caught up in his duties that he began to love himself. What would have happened had he had a choice? What would have happened if the fallen had a choice to stay or go. There was no choice. They didn't obey, so they were cast out.

"Before I created humans, I told myself to never do that again. To allow choice and reason. To experience true love that is authentic and real and not a programmed reaction. The pain comes that they may walk away and choose another. The pain comes when I have done everything for them, and yet they still complain and walk away. The pain comes when I beg and plead for them to choose Me, and yet they find Me unworthy."

"Master, You are worthy. Nothing is more worthy than You."

"Thank you, Ramiel. That is why it hurts. This hurt and love you feel, I have felt since their creation. I created the garden, and they chose not to obey. I rescued them from Egypt, and they chose not to obey and to complain. I wanted to be their King and to be with them, and yet they wanted Saul. I wanted to be their God and to commune with them personally, yet they wanted their priests and not Me. I gave them their law that they asked for. The kings they requested and the prophets that they killed. I fed them while they wandered. I gave them drink when they thirsted, and I died and came back for them when they needed Me to. Yet they still chose to fall away. And I still love them so much that I will allow them to do it.

"I have given them everything that they could ask for and more, and yet they still choose to fall away. I am their scapegoat when they need a villain. I am their excuse when they won't accept responsibility, and they even try to make Me their one-night stand when all I ask for is a committed relationship. I allow them these opportunities and chances out of love. This pain you feel, I feel and will feel thousands of more times today and every day until my return."

Ramiel's eyes are opened even further in the spiritual realm as he sees the Master having this same conversation with thousands of other protectors flying through the heavens as they continue their journey home.

"You were given a chance to see and experience some of the love and responsibility that I have for my creation. You were given Emily to watch over because I knew you would fall in love with her just like I have."

"I do love her. That's why it hurts so much. I gave everything to protect her. I don't know what else I could have done other than stopping that vehicle to protect her."

"It wasn't your job to stop that. It was out of your hands. That young lady had the opportunity to drive normally and safely, yet she chose to text a friend while intoxicated and speeding through the city. She chose that, and her choice had consequences. They reap what they sow.

"Emily's parents had the opportunity to choose me. They both had multiple occasions to join with me, and I to join with them. But they didn't, and I am not going to force it.

"Everyone is too busy now doing nothing. Signing up for activities with meaningless recognition, going to every event that's possible, choosing to follow Me by online status only. Where is the intimacy in that?

"I beg and plead for it. I died for it, and yet they still choose death. And yet I still love them and allow it. I love them more than they will ever know, and I show it to them on a daily basis, and yet they don't love Me back. All I will do is love them and wait for them in return."

"I'm so sorry, Master. I can't imagine the pain or anguish and heartbreak."

"Thank you, Ramiel. It's okay. It's all worth it for the ones that choose Me. Oh, what a celebration we have when that day happens. I go down and greet them and commune with them. Angels rejoice and sing praise for what happens. It's louder and more electric than the biggest thunderstorm I allow to happen on earth. There are no words to describe how I feel when they choose me. When they could do anything else and choose anything else, they see Me and choose me. It's more beautiful to Me than all of heaven," the Master gets a little choked up thinking about how He feels when that beautiful process occurs. "Ramiel, until your next assignment, I will put you on the rejoice team. This way you can see and experience a taste of that love being reciprocated. There is nothing else like it."

"I would like that. Sir, I just wanted You to know one last time that I truly do love Emily and did everything I could to protect her. I'm so sorry that she couldn't make it to her time of choosing."

The Master leans back in and pulls Ramiel toward Him for a hug.

"It wasn't your fault. You did an extraordinary and stunning job. I love you, Ramiel. I love you very much," the Master whispers into his ear as they embrace.

"I love you too," he replies as they reminisce over Emily and arrive back home.

Chapter 13

"Your daughter broke both arms, three ribs, and her left tibia. She has a concussion from being knocked out and hitting her head several times. The good news is that we don't see any other brain trauma currently," the doctor explains to Bill and Nancy as they arrive at the hospital emergency room. They are beyond worried and scared for the well-being of their child as tears, thoughts of fear, and brokenness flood their minds.

"She is in recovery right now. We were able to calm her down and stabilize her. She was very excited and scared when she woke up. She was unconscious upon EMT arrival but woke up during the ambulance ride back."

"Where is she? I want to see her. Where is my baby?" Nancy asks as she sobs and turns for comfort into Bill's arms.

"Ma'am, I need you to calm down. I understand this is a scary time for you right now, but there is good news. Those injuries are all that we can find at the moment. They are fixable, and with the proper care, she will recover and live a normal physical life.

"The staff is moving her to a room so we can monitor her for the next few days to make sure she has no brain damage or swelling. The major concern right now is her mental well-being more than her physical. She is the only survivor from the vehicle and—"

Nancy plummets to the floor, disregarding any other news heading her way as she realizes her good friend and entire family are dead. It hadn't occurred to her yet about Becky and her family until just then. She weeps and mourns over the whole ordeal. Her body shakes, contracts, and expands repeatedly and almost violently as she processes everything that has happened. The mental and physical well-being of her daughter and the passing of a wonderful friend and family are too much to bear for the moment, and her body is trying to survive the load. Thoughts of how her daughter may react to hear her best friend has died right beside her causes another monsoon of tears to fall.

Bill, feeling hopeless and helpless, kneels down and cautiously rubs his wife's back. A few tears fall as the same thoughts run through his mind, but all he can do at this moment is to try and console Nancy. His natural reaction is to shut down, absorb and process later. This moment only lasts a few minutes as the staff helps the couple off the floor and guides them back into the depths of the hospital to see their little girl.

"Again, we understand that this is very hard for you. However, your daughter needs you to be strong right now. You need to be strong for her and not overreact or lose control in front of her. She is heavily medicated and sedated, so she won't try and move as we need her to be as still as possible. Be careful not to touch—"

"Just shut up and let me see my little girl," Nancy interrupts and stares down the escorting nurse as if she were a mother bear, and the nurse stood between her and her cub.

During this entire time that Sara has been in the hospital, Sariel has been battling. Upon arriving at the entrance, he fought off a small horde of fallen that have made the ambulance driveway a buffet of sorts. Entering inside and riding on top of Sara's body, Sariel has gallantly fought off all the fallen that have reached for her spirit as he uses her gurney like a steed in battle. During the examination and the addressing of her wounds, he flew around the room like lighting from the sky and smote the fallen that used doctors and nurses to enter the area, as well as any free-roaming fallen in his vicinity.

He has fought tirelessly, using the battle as a distraction and almost peace of mind instead of focusing on the condition of his little Sara. Every time he glances at her, he sees her brokenness, which encourages him to swing harder and fly faster.

This charade goes on for thirty-two hours straight. Sariel should be exhausted, but he isn't. His adrenaline and Sara's physical presentation give him the boost that he needs to keep on going.

Over the course of the thirty-two hours, Sara managed to wake up twice. Both times she was drowsy and so heavily medicated that she could not speak properly. Bill and Nancy haven't left her side as they remain in her room. Both of them are still knowers, and the fallen take advantage of it and continuously use them as a portal to attack Sariel and Sara.

At the start of the thirty-third hour, Sara eventually wakes up and is able to stay awake for more than five minutes. Doctors and parents begin to ask questions about her health and memory.

"Where's Emily?" is the only response that she gives them as that is all she can think about. "Mom, where's Emily?"

"Baby, listen to me okay? Emily didn't make it. She's with Jesus in heaven. She's no longer in—"

She's interrupted by a scream of pain and remorse beyond that of a physical nature. Sara begins to quake under the pressure of tears trying to leave her at one time that her physical well-being grows beyond her control. The doctors immediately administer medicine to calm her down, so she won't physically hurt herself, causing further damage. Within a few minutes, she is asleep again. Her parents console one another as they continue to stand guard over their little girl.

Sariel hears for the first time that Emily is gone causing Ramiel to be gone as well. He hasn't had time to process or think on the others as he has been preoccupied since pulling Sara from the wreckage. A fire ignites in his eyes as he hears the news. The idiotic fallen laugh and mock him as he learns their fates. Sariel transforms into a hurricane of fire and death as he spins, slashes, and destroys everything spiritual in the room that is not of the Master. He cries for the loss of Emily with each dominant rotation. He mourns for his friend as he hopes to never experience what Ramiel has. Each swing of the blades fly faster and with more precision as the absence of his friend and his little one swim through his mind.

Forty-eight more hours pass since they have learned of their friend's fate, and Sara has calmed down enough to quietly sit in bed and act nonresponsive. Bill and Nancy believe it would be a good idea to stream Emily's family funeral so Sara could see her friend in pictures of life and love. They wonder if hearing beautiful stories and memories of her friend may give her a better mental image of Emily than the current one of death and brokenness. They are doing whatever they can to get her to move, communicate, or even react to something as Sara has continued to sit like a statue in a garden, motionless and present only for others.

Bill attends the service and streams through his phone to Nancy, who is bedside with her daughter.

"How do you begin a service with so much loss and inspire hope?" the pastor speaks trying to keep a composed profile but clearly presents a flustered and hurt shepherd. "I can only say, 'God. I've known Emily and her mother, Becky, for quite some time. They always sat over there in that pew. They were some of the good ones. They never fell asleep during any of my sermons. They listened and watched, sang and said hello to any nearby person. They were sweet people.' The good Lord then brought along the head of the house, Ralph, as he joined us not too long ago."

While the service is being streamed, fallen activity picks up in the room. The enemy begins to flood in as if they too are trying to listen to the phone. Through Nancy, nearby nurses, and the roaming fallen in the hallways, the demonic fill the room. Sariel has his hands full as he connects and clashes with the entering fallen. Sara doesn't say a word, but sits there stoic and frozen as she glances at the phone from time to time. She primarily looks straight ahead and just listens.

"This family were good people. Salt of the earth people. They were kind, helpful, thoughtful, and loved the Lord. This is a hard time now for our congregation, but I know they loved God. I know He was their Lord."

Fallen begin to cackle and laugh as they hear the false testimony that everyone wants to believe. They look toward Sara and see that she is currently watching the phone. As if commanded, they immediately turn their full attention toward Sariel and grow in their boldness as they try to hold him down by each limb. Fallen are smitten one after another but slowly gain ground as they grab one leg and then the other.

More fallen pour into the room, continuing to use Sara's mom and the other available portals on the hospital floor. Eventually, they come to a point where they have Sariel held down on his back, hindering the use of his wings, as well as having all four limbs pinned. The amount of fallen in the room create a black hole of darkness. Sariel is able to shake free only momentarily and destroy a few fallen before being returned to his defeated position.

"The Lord giveth and the Lord taketh away. The Lord took away good people, but the good news is that the Lord took them home. That great revival service in the arena was a spectacular time of prayer and spiritual growth. I can only imagine how excited the family was to leave that arena and to enter His heavenly grace. We still pray for the recovery of Sara as I see her father in attendance."

"God loves you?" the fallen begin to whisper in Sara's ear. "If He loved you so much, why did He kill your best friend and her parents? Why is He punishing you by making you stay here? How is that love?"

Sariel sees and hears what is going on and begins to scream in protest, "No!" He manages to get up again but is unable to move closer to Sara as the presence of the enemy is completely overwhelming at the moment. Every swing and movement of his being is met by darkness and death, as if the fallen had become a spider web and are not allowing their victim to escape.

"How does God show you His love? By killing your friend's family, even after you went to a service honoring Him. That's what you were doing, right? You were at church for your God, and then this happened. *Tsk, tsk, tsk,* that does not sound like love to me.

"By the way, have you told your parents yet that it's your fault that Emily's mom is dead?" Sara continues to watch the phone as tears begin to fall from her eyes. "I mean she unbuckled her belt for you. She would possibly still be alive if you could have just held on to your tablet. But your loving God didn't give you the grip you needed, and He took them from you. What a shame."

"No!" Sariel screams again as he slashes, tries to spin, fights with everything in his being, but still is stuck by the mass of enemies in the room, unable to gain any ground whatsoever. Still, Sariel fights on, not giving up.

As the dance and deception continue to take place, a light interrupts their activities and begins to shine in the mind of Sara, turning all attention toward it, like flies to a flame. The light starts out as small as a grape, but quickly grows to the size of a large cantaloupe. Its purity and sparkle are equal to a bright reflection through a dazzling diamond.

The fallen stop whispering and drop their arms. Sariel does the same as all parties witness up close the birth of a choosing moment. It's at this time that Sara makes a decision. She watches the phone as her dad sweeps the phone left to right catching pictures of the lost. As the camera pans across Emily's father, then to Emily, and then to her mother, she makes her choice. How could God let her friend die and how can she ever be forgiven for killing her best friend's mom? Sariel bows his head, falls to his knees, and weeps. His protection covering over Sara fades away as she is now a knower.

Sara's mom continues to stream the phone right in the face of her daughter, not knowing the destruction that it's caused. She believes the tears shed by her daughter are tears of love lost as she sees her friend's portrait. She doesn't realize they are tears of guilt and shame.

Sariel continues to cry and weep. He feels a difference in atmosphere take place, so he raises his head and looks to see his new surroundings. He finds himself flying home through the celestial galaxies. The Master is also in flight beside him and places His hands on Sariel's shoulders. They embrace and mourn as another loved one chooses to know rather than follow.

Chapter 14

"What do I do next?"

"You wait for my command. I have something planned for you, but it's not ready just yet. Just wait for your next assignment from Me. I will personally come and get you when the time is right. Don't go too far from my throne room."

"Yes, sir," Sariel answers, turns, and exits the doorway of the throne room.

He is numb from what just transpired in that hospital room. He does feel the effects of home begin to calm his spirit with each step; but still, the sting of her choice has left a paralyzing numbness to his core.

He's never experienced anything like this before; to him, it feels as if he submerged into a frozen lake and his body has adapted to the pain and stiffness. He knows what he is feeling isn't right, but he doesn't know what to do about it. He heeds the Master's command to obey and wait. He doesn't want to merely stand around, so he begins to walk.

Angels have known loss and sadness in heaven before. Heaven is not for angels like it is for humans. They have lost brothers and have experienced pain there. Sariel feels as if Sara is gone forever. The disconnection of her spirit to his has left a void that he is not used to. She is now a knower, and he is hurt.

Sariel begins to walk the streets of gold as he doesn't want to merely stand still. Heaven is covered from head to toe in light. The light emitting from the throne room causes all darkness to be nonexistent. Even buildings and vegetation that surround the throne room are without shadow as its presence is not permitted. Structures towering higher than the human eye can see litter both sides of the streets.

Rubies, emeralds, pearls, diamonds, and all other forms of rock and stone that humans hold as value are used here as building material. All paths are formed by streets of gold as a man's precious commodity is used as asphalt. The colors and array of the splendor of heaven are beyond compare. The only word that fits the description of this place is the Master. While flying to an assignment, Ramiel sees his friend and flies over to chat.

"Sariel, how's it going? You doing okay? Wait, what's wrong?" Ramiel asks as he places his right hand on Sariel's shoulder, bringing him to a sudden halt. He sees his friend is in pain and wants to help.

"What? Oh, hey, Ramiel. How are you?" Sariel whispers his response as he begrudgingly lifts his head to make eye contact with his friend.

"I'm great, but what's going on with you? Is everything okay? Did Sara not make it? Did she grow old and become a follower, and you're dazed from the ride? Come on, what's going on? Why are you acting like this?" he takes his hand that's on Sariel's shoulder and nudges him ever so slightly.

"Grow old? What do you mean, I just saw you not even a week ago. Just a few days, in fact," he shrugs his face in disapproval and annoyance as the questions seem out of place.

"Hey, have you forgotten where you are currently? Time doesn't work the same here, you know that. It took me some time as well to adjust being back, but I'm good now." Ramiel motions over his being, presenting himself much differently than the last time the two of them were together. He immediately understands his friend's sorrow as he recalls that city street and the state of affairs they were in. He changes his tone to be light and soft before continuing.

"So, I take it that Sara passed since we just saw each other. I'm so sorry my friend." Ramiel lifts his arms again toward his friend to welcome him for an embrace. Sariel unconsciously accepts as his body naturally moves in for support. Ramiel pulls him in toward his chest with a tight grip as if his own life force would penetrate his friend and bring him joy. "Give it a few hours, and you'll begin to feel better again."

"No, Sara did not die, Ramiel. She did something worse. She chose to be a knower." Sariel separates himself at arm's length from Ramiel, as if he is the cause of the decision and the leprosy of her choice would rub off on him. He then drops his head and begins to weep.

"That's it? That's what the fuss is over? Hey, she's still alive and was able to choose," Ramiel is surprised and disappointed in his friend's sorrow. He puts his hands on his hips like an angry parent would preparing for an ill-faded explanation.

"Yeah, that's it, and she chose wrong. I messed up, and now she's gone," he continues in his self-pity.

"Gone, really? Did she die in your hands? Did you pray for her as she slipped away? Did you sit there and watch as the fallen took her soul from her body? Did that happen? Did it my friend?" Ramiel gets emotional, and his voice cracks as he finishes recalling the events that had happened to his Emily.

"No. No, it didn't, but it might as well have. She's gone, just like Emily, and I failed," Sariel looks his friend square in the eyes as if his stare might explain the guilt and loss that he is currently feeling.

"Get over yourself. It's not over. Far from it. Your Sara is still alive. Emily is dead and gone forever. She's not coming back. There is no hope for her. Sara at least still has hope."

"You don't know what you're talking about. I saw what happened. I saw her choose, and her light of choice came, and then it became dark. I couldn't fix it. I couldn't stop it. There were so many fallen in that room. I couldn't advance even an inch. I was helpless—"

"Shut your mouth," Ramiel interrupts the pity party before Sariel could say another word. "This weakness and misguided sorrow are not allowed here. You are not allowed to accept the words that you just said. This is glory, this is heaven, this is home. You have no idea what you're saying. You need to talk to the Master. He will help you. He helped me when I got back."

"I was just there, and he told me to wait. So, I'm waiting like I was commanded to do," Sariel sarcastically waves his arm in front of his chest, lowers his head, and resumes his self-loathing.

"Stop with all of the dramatics. This isn't like you. As long as she is alive, she will always have the choice to turn and go the other way. Emily doesn't have that option anymore. I can't wait for her to choose and to bring me back as protector again. I'm done. Your feeling sorry for yourself when you did nothing wrong, and you still have hope. You need to look at the big picture and put your big boy wings on."

"I failed. What do you mean I did nothing wrong!"

"Is she still alive?"

"Yes."

"Then there is hope. Where there is life, there is hope. Listen to what I am saying. I'm tired of repeating myself. Actually, you know what, this may help," Ramiel crosses his arms and shoots a hip out and sideways to get comfortable. "Tell me everything that happened after the accident. Lay it on me, give your all."

"All right, fine. You asked, so I'll tell," Sariel begins to look off and beyond their location. Not at the beauty and majesty of heaven, but he peers into that hospital room of pain and anguish. "I can't tell you how long I fought without a break, but I know it was several days. I waged war against any fallen that might enter the room that Sara was in. I didn't let a single fallen touch her. I don't remember if I have ever fought so valiantly in my existence before. As if my own eternity rested on the outcome.

"Time passed, and Sara began to heal. She came to a point where she was able to stay awake for multiple hours. The third day in the hospital was the funeral for Emily's family, so her parents thought it would be best to live stream the service for Sara. Her father went to the ceremony and they communicated through the devices.

"The service was awful. It was all a lie. By this time, I had heard that Emily had passed as well as her parents, and I knew what would have occurred. The fallen also heard the message of deceit spewing from the phone and immediately began to swell in number. As if each deceitful word multiplied their existence, they became too many to even move. They pinned me down and began working on her.

"By the time I was able to get up and even try to fight back, she was gone. Her light came and we all stopped. No one on either side moved as we watched the process. She made her decision and then I was headed back home. The Master hugged me and told me to wait for my next assignment from Him. Then you happened," Sariel brings his eye contact back to his friend, looking at him for an apology since he clearly believes the story validates his current mood.

"Wow, that's incredible. Everything sounds incredible. I am so happy for you. I truly can't believe it. Congratulations," Ramiel is overjoyed and reacts in the exact opposite fashion of what his friend expected.

"Hold up. What? Why are you acting like this? What was good about what I just told you?"

"Okay, this is really the last time I will repeat myself. First, she's alive, so there is hope. Second, the Master told you to wait. That means He knows something.

"When I was headed home, we had a long and beautiful talk. We both cried and felt the loss. We embraced and strengthened each other. It was a wonderful moment. He then told me that I could be a part of the rejoice team after people had chosen to follow. I've already been a part of eleven, and He is right. The sensation and joy that comes when they choose to follow Him is unlike any other love or experience I have ever been a part of. I'm beginning to understand and know why He did what He did. True love is letting the other love you back and not forcing or making them do it. And, man, when they do, it's exhilarating," Ramiel's entire demeanor expresses pure joy as he breaks eye contact and stares off into the cosmos replaying the latest salvation experience he was apart of.

"What are you saying, Ramiel?" Sariel perks up as he begins to truly listen to what his friend has been saying all of this time. The sorrow starts to fade, and hope starts to spring from inside of Sariel.

"Oh, my goodness, brother. Why are you being so dense? Let me make this as simple as possible for you. Sara still has time. The Master told you to wait. He obviously knows something is coming and that is why He gave you that command. He knows all, all the time. It's beyond our comprehension, but not His.

"Why didn't He give you another job yet? Order and obedience are essential for Him. He wouldn't let you just do nothing. Something must be coming. Don't forget, time is different here. You're not on earth anymore. In the blink of an eye and you could miss a millennium or just a day. Time is not counted here like it is on earth."

Sariel immediately begins to smile as his negative attitude completely fades, and he begins to understand the words his friend has been sharing with him.

"You really think so? I never thought of that, but you're right. Something is about to happen, isn't there? What if something is happening right now? I need to get back to the throne room. I need to—"

Sariel turns to head back to where he just came from when he is suddenly stopped as his face sinks into the Master's chest. He retracts his body from the Master and, with a grin from ear to ear, addresses him, "I am so sorry, sir. I was just heading back your way, and then I—"

"Sariel, it's okay. It's all okay, my friend," the master pauses and smiles at Ramiel in approval, as if He had been standing there listening this entire time. "It's time now. I have something for you to do. Can you please come with Me?"

Chapter 15

"Are you sure you're okay with this? If not, just text me, and we'll come home. I will drive back here so fast you won't have time to hang up the phone. Just let me know if this gets to be too much. You're not as young as you once were mom," Sara laughs as she hands over little Emily.

"We will be just fine. In fact, we're excited, right honey?" She looks over her shoulder to yell at Bill who is sitting on the couch, catching up on the sports news of the day.

"Yeah, yeah, this will be great. We're gonna licker her up, give her three bags of powdered sugar, and let her play in honey so she gets sticky everywhere. It's gonna be a great time," Bill laughs as he is obviously joking about the night's activities while never breaking eye contact with his sports program.

"Now I know you're just trying to be funny, but please don't do any of what you just said. You sure you can handle this, mom? Dad looks like he is going to be very helpful."

"I raised you, didn't I? And you turned out okay."

"That's what I'm afraid of."

"Oh, honey, come on, just stop it. Me and Emily are going to have a blast. We have her milk bottle, plenty of diapers, clothes, and her favorite toys. We're gonna play for a little bit, and then I will give her a bath so she will be clean for church tomorrow. Everything is going to be just fine. Her crib is set up, and I've been yearning for her to have a sleepover in it. Let me enjoy this, okay?

"Why don't you run and get in the car with your husband, and you guys go to your party. We will see you in the morning for the early service."

"Yeah, we may not make it. It depends on how late tonight turns out to be. Either way, I will come get her. But seriously, message me if anything comes up, okay?"

"I will, I will. Just go. You're ruining my grandma mojo."

"Okay, fine, just one last kiss."

Sara leans in to give Emily kisses on the cheeks and on her forehead. She whispers nonsense only she understands into her daughter's ear, but Emily reacts with smiles and with a sense of understanding and love. This happens for a few more seconds until Sara raises her head and kisses her mom's cheek.

"Thank you, guys, so much. I know Peter really appreciates it, and we could use the night out."

"It is our pleasure. Honestly, you're not gonna know what to do with all the sleep you're going to get, so enjoy it. Have fun and be safe, we will see you in the morning." She kisses her daughter back and then turns to walk toward the living room and away from the front door.

"Bye, dad. Thanks again."

"No problem, sweetie. You two have fun tonight. See ya tomorrow at church."

"Yeah, uh-huh. See ya." She brushes off the idea of church as it's not been a priority for her since that day in the hospital. She's had a few close encounters through the years with the Master, but her guilt about Emily's mom takes over, and she just won't let that go.

And with that sarcastic reply, Sara turns, shuts the door, and heads toward the family SUV and Peter, her husband of two and a half years.

Peter and Sara actually met through their parents who are friends from church. Peter's mom moved to the area five years ago and ran into Sara's mom at a church function. They hit it off and started planning their kids' wedding together. A few months into their friendship, Peter and Sara met, and the rest is history.

"All set?"

"Yeah, we're good." Sara fastens her seatbelt as she settles in and shuts the door.

"How about you? Are you going to be okay? This is your first night out without her. It's a big step, and I'm proud of you."

"I'm fine. I just want to enjoy tonight. I want to relax and not run for a spill or diaper change or to cuddle. I jus—"

"What if I want to cuddle?" He reaches for Sara's thigh and hand as he gazes into her eyes.

"Really? Is that all you think about? Last time we cuddled on a similar night to this, she happened. Plus, I haven't slept in weeks. No cuddling, just adult time and sleep. You can cuddle with yourself. Now, can we please go?" Sara leans over and kisses her husband after she rejects him. As if that action will make up for any inaction later this evening.

"Oh, okay. This is gonna be great," he responds with a valley-girl-like accent and begins to drive away.

"Oh, hey, when are we supposed to pick her up?"

"I told mom to text me if anything comes up, but if everything goes to plan, we will make the exchange tomorrow at church."

"Okay cool. I'm kinda excited for tomorrow myself. It should be good."

"About church?" Sara responds as if surprised by his response as she applies more makeup in the mirror.

"Yeah, it has been getting good lately. The pastor has been on a kick, and I like it. Who knows, maybe one day it will stick for you."

"Yup, maybe one day."

"Oh come on, you have to let go of the accident. Heck, it was a miracle you survived at all." Peter quickly wishes he could retract his last words as he knows they are a sore spot and cause for argument with his wife.

"We've talked about this. I go to church to please my parents and for the coffee and meeting people. If the miracles were true and all that stuff was real, then my friend would have survived also. It's not a miracle I'm here. It's a cruel and messed-up joke. They died, and I didn't. That's not a miracle," she stares him straight through as she finishes her statement, not wanting to reveal her true guilt about Emily's mother.

"Listen, I'm not trying to ruin our night or piss you off. But that stuff is real. I told you what I saw with my grandma. Bad things happen to good people all the time. That doesn't mean He's a bad god or anything. It just means something crappy happened."

"Maybe another time, okay? But tonight were headed to a party. I'm having a couple of drinks and so will you. Let's just focus on that right now. We can talk god another time or whatever. I just don't want to right now, okay?"

"Yeah, babe, that's fine, I'm not trying to make you mad. I just like what I've been hearing lately at church. Plus, that group of older ladies loves Emily and us, and you know I love them and their candies. They're always dropping little hints or like little gut questions to me when I ask for a mint or caramel. I don't know. I've just been thinking about it lately. That's all. I won't bring it up again tonight."

"Thank you."

Peter is a suspicious knower. He wants to believe, but the lack of spiritual desire from his wife and the commitment to a spiritual relationship with the Master has kept him on the wayside. If he would only open his own eyes to his own soul and not use others as an excuse or crutch, he would see the Master is calling to him. Not only on Sunday's, but He calls every day and for an intimate love.

The love Peter has for his daughter makes him question regularly just how much God could love him. Emily's smile and innocence drive him to be a better man and father, but he allows life and his wife's struggle to get in the way of his search for more. Eventually, the vehicle pulls up to its destination, and the couple exits.

"Are you ready?" Peter asks his wife as he clicks the security feature on his key fob. "It should be fun."

"Yeah, no texts from mom yet, so all is well. I'm ready to relax and enjoy our first night out."

They give each other a quick kiss and hold hands as they march toward their friend's door. The entourage of people are scattered throughout the home, but most of them are in the kitchen eating or hanging out in the back, talking on the deck. They enter inside and greet friends, grab food, take a glass of wine, and relax.

Hours go by as the happy couple consumes food, alcohol, and the lackluster need to change diapers. Sara and Peter are thoroughly enjoying themselves. However, the idea of escape from their little one has washed away as each other person present wants to see pictures, talk stories, and compare battle scars of parenthood.

Sara stops drinking wine after her fourth glass. She tells Peter he can continue and she will drive home since he drove them to the party. The festivities continue late into the night, and Sara and Peter eventually make their way back out of the home's entrance around 1:15 a.m. They wish everyone a pleasant remainder of the weekend as they climb inside their SUV to head home.

"That was fun, that was fun, that was a great time. I had a great time, honey," Peter repeats himself as the alcohol tries to take command of his speech.

"Yeah, that was a great break. I didn't realize how much I needed that. I'm just glad everything is going well with Emily, and mom didn't need us to come get her."

"That would have sucked. That would have been terrible, absolutely terrible. That girl would be so grounded if she had acted up. I mean she would be in major trouble. No boobies. That would have been a rightful punishment.

"And not your old friend but our daughter. I mean our little Emily, not your Emily. She and I would sit in solitaire together and complain about it. Yup, that's what would have happened. I would have sat in a corner with my daughter and complained about the lack of boobies." Peter turns his head and leans against the glass as its cool touch is a comfort to him. He closes his eyes and begins to drift asleep.

"Babe, oh my god, are you drunk? I can't believe you sometimes."

"I love you, too, babe. I love you so much," he whispers as the heat of his breath stampedes across the glass, leaving its mark.

"I didn't say that. Never mind, it's not worth fighting over at one in the morning with a drunk guy," she whispers that last part to herself as she doesn't want to express her pain or make a scene. It's just that most mentions of her childhood friend is a reminder of loss and shame for her.

As Sara spirals down a rabbit hole of guilt caused by her husband's intoxicated remarks, she is unaware of the deer that is in the middle of the road. Somehow, moments before impact, she sees the four-legged beast and quickly overcompensates, causing the vehicle to swerve, spin, and hit a small tree.

Chapter 16

"Are you okay? Are you okay? Come on, tell me. Are you ok?" Peter emphatically overcompensates with emotion as he has become almost immediately sober. He jumps out of his seat and makes his way to the driver side door to check on his wife.

"Yeah, I'm fine. I'm good. I just didn't see that deer until the last second. Are you okay?" Sara rubs her head trying to erase the pain of hitting it with her own hand on the impact.

She closes her eyes for a split-second but finds herself eyes wide open in another place. She is in the past, and she's witnessing the accident take place so many years ago in a dream-like world covered in a rustic tint. The angle is that of an onlooker from the sidewalk; she is able to see the young girl crash directly into them. She cannot move to go help; she can only stand. No noise or movement; she is as a statue watching. She sees her friend's side of the vehicle disappear into itself as the vehicle rolls and rotates through the air. She watches as Emily's mom is thrown like a Frisbee from a toddler—no direction or aim, merely achieving maximum height and then the eventual crash.

"Oh my god!" Sara is finally able to scream as the body makes contact with the pavement.

"What… what is it? Are you hurt? What's wrong?" Peter frantically unbuckles his seat belt to be able to console and review Sara's condition.

"Oh my god, I did that, I did that. That was my fault. Oh my god." Sara begins to shake with fear, pain, and remorse.

What she is unable to see are the fallen currently crawling on top of her and sucking and licking her as if she were a dessert coffee covered in cream. They cover her with their long tongues filled with the stench of decay and rottenness. The fear that she is exhuming from her body is feeding the fallen, and they are lapping it up like a dog at his favorite toilet bowl. Since neither Sara nor Peter are followers, they have no assistance with the matter and are at the mercy of the spiritual jackals.

"Babe, it was just an accident. We're going to be fine. Quit freaking out and tell me you're okay." Peter reaches over her body and unbuckles her seatbelt. "Let me check you out really quick." He then combs over her body looking for any swelling or cuts of any kind. Currently, he only sees the bruise forming on her left eye that her hand caused when it smacked her at impact.

Sara sits still for the examination, allowing him free reign to move and manipulate her body. She goes into a small state of shock as the past replays in her mind like a bad movie at a late hour.

Back inside her head, she watches the wreck complete itself. The car lands and she is unable to see herself or her side of the vehicle. After her scream, she unlocked the ability to move in this horrible and dream-state world. She starts to move toward the building that is directly beside the overturned vehicle. On her way, she witnesses Emily's hand fall and hang down like a demented piece of decor. She only sees one hand, but it's lifeless and it's swaying like a butchered hog being pushed on a meat hook. She grabs her mouth and freezes in place, trying to stop herself from throwing up. Meanwhile, she is able to understand that in the physical world her husband is still talking to her and moving her around.

She stands for a few more seconds just staring at the hand swaying back and forth. Without her knowing how or ability, she finds herself gliding over to her destination. She stops a little over ten yards away and has perfect line of sight of the vehicle and the building. She sees glass moving and her seatbelt jerk. She looks closer, and as she leans in, she is greeted by the fall and thumb of her body hitting the roof of the vehicle, that was now placed underneath her.

She follows a piece of glass that is moving, like something was standing on top of it. She can't see anything there, but the physical presentation happening with that glass is grabbing her full attention. Suddenly, in three long and swift movements, the glass is against the building wall. Sara's attention then moves beyond the glass, and she sees her body lying on the sidewalk. She stands upright and motions her head around, trying to spot the hero that pulled her from the wreckage.

As she stands erect, she sees a glimpse of a face for only the briefest of moments, but she sees a face. It's the same face that she thought had greeted her that day so long ago. In a blink of an eye, it's gone. She bends back over to see if it's moved inside the vehicle when she is then greeted by the gaze of her husband.

She blinks and then is released from the power of that nightmare and is brought back to her SUV. She blinks a few more times and sees she's staring straight at her husband's nose. Beyond his face, she can see that no airbags were deployed, and no smoke is rising. Her current accident is not even close or on par with the one that she was a part of so many years ago. This accident is a fender bender at best.

"Babe, what's wrong? Talk to me." Peter grabs her hand and holds it tight.

"What did I do?" What did I do, Peter?"

"You swerved and missed a deer but got the tree," he chuckles as his adrenaline is still racing through him.

"I don't mean that. I mean, why are we here? Why am I here? My best friend in the whole world, my whole childhood is summed up by alcohol and driving. Why am I here? Am I so stupid that I did the same thing that I have hated for so long? Am I that girl?" Sara tenses up and sits up straight as if to make her point.

"Whoa, whoa, babe. No, you're not that girl. We're fine. Your fine. It was just a deer. You didn't hit anyone. You didn't even hit the deer. Look, no one is around us. We're alone," Peter motions with his hand to the exterior of the cockpit.

"That's not what I'm talking about," She shrinks back into the seat as words fall from her mouth. "I'm talking about why did I drive after the party? Why did we escape to even go to a party? Why aren't we with our daughter? What if we died? We would have left her. I can't be responsible for that, too. I thought I loved her too much to let that happen."

"Hey now, what do you mean 'you can't be responsible for that, too'? What are you talking about, Sara?"

"You really want to know?"

"Yes, of course I do. What's going on?"

"I'm the reason Emily's mom died. I killed Becky. It was my fault she flew out the window." Like opening a dam, her face begins to release any liquid that it once held back. The pressure of the words spoken and guilt held on to for so many years causes her to drop her head and sink into herself.

"Come on, stop this right now. You're either still tipsy or you hit your head harder than I thought. You didn't kill her. The accident did," Peter says anything he can to get his wife to calm down.

"I dropped my tablet. I dropped my tablet on the floor of the car, and she unbuckled to get it for me. I lived, and she was thrown from the vehicle like a rag doll. Now you tell me. If I was able to live, wouldn't she have lived as well since it wasn't our side that was hit?" Tears continue to fall down her face. They bring pain but also release a heavy load as she has never told that to anyone before this night.

"That's absurd. No way it's your fault. No, no, not at all. She died because of the stupid girl who was not only drunk, but also texting at the same time. You can't blame yourself for that."

"You don't know that. You don't know if she would have lived or not. We will never know because she's gone. And tonight, I almost did the same thing that you just called stupid. I could have left Emily and could have taken you with me."

She collapses and falls halfway out of her door and onto Peter's chest. The late hour, the trauma of the accident, and the memory of her past are too much for her. Peter wraps his hands around her and just holds her. He doesn't say anything else; he only holds her and kisses her on her cheek and forehead every few seconds.

Eventually, a few minutes pass and he offers to switch places with her and to drive them home. She agrees. He helps guide her around the front of the car while assessing the damage. To his happy surprise, the exterior is mostly in good shape, with only a few scrapes and dents from the tree. He climbs in and pulls away. They make it home, and he carries her to bed.

They are awakened by the sound of his phone alarm going off. Peter was able to sleep rather soundly, but Sara tossed and turned all through the remaining hours. She eventually gave up hope of rest around 5:30 a.m. and just laid on her side. She even witnessed the sunrise through her windows, but was only able to stare at it and not enjoy that beautiful piece of creation. All night she attacked herself and was beating herself up for what she believes she did and caused.

She gets out of bed and turns off Peter's alarm and then heads into the kitchen to make coffee. A few minutes later. Peter joins her and gives her a hug.

"Did last night really happen, or was that a terrible dream? I really want it to be a dream."

"No, babe, it happened. I'm sorry." She rubs his back and kisses his cheek. She then separates herself from his hold and motions toward the life liquid.

"Babe, you don't need to apologize. Everything is going to be fine. It's all fine." He follows her lead, and they prepare their cups. "We need to finish these quickly and get ready for church, okay?"

"Are you serious? Today is not a good day for us to go to church. I'm sore, I didn't sleep at all, I'm just not in the mood to fake it today, okay?"

"It doesn't matter. We need to pick up Emily, and you told your parents last night that you would see them there today. If we don't show up, they will think something happened, and your mom will march straight over here anyway. Let's just do this. You will be fine. Put some makeup over your eye, and you'll be fine."

She doesn't feel like arguing—she doesn't feel like doing any-thing—so she caves in. They drink their coffee and prepare for the service.

Time passes, and they head toward church. Sara's phone goes off with a text from her mom. It's a picture of Emily in a cute little new dress. It's captioned "see you soon, mommy." This brightens her mood, and she becomes eager to see her child.

They pull into church ahead of the rush and join her parents. She takes Emily into her arms and begins to kiss her little princess all over. Sara's mother notices her eye and asks about the bruise, but she waves it off as an accident. Then her mom's eyes widen, and she looks over toward Peter, as if implying that he attacked her. She shakes her head no, and then motions with her hand as if she were drinking from a glass, and then smacks her head as if trying to explain what happened through charades. Her mother catches the subtle clue and rolls her eyes.

Sara lowers her head at just the motion of her drinking. Shame and regret creep over her but don't settle. The thoughts come and go, like a leaf in the wind. What she didn't realize was that the big five and Emily's protector had taken care of the uninvited fallen, and that's why the regret didn't stay.

The service begins, and the praise and worship start. The songs are beautiful, but Sara is fixated on her daughter. She uses Emily as an excuse and plays with her instead of participating. Eventually, that part of the service ends, announcements are made, and the pastor takes the pulpit. The title of his message is *He Loves Me No Matter What*.

Peter sees an uneasiness come over Sara as she prepares Emily's bag to excuse herself from the service. He quickly catches the notion that she needs to hear this message. He grabs the bag and takes Emily into his arms. He mouths to Sara that he's got her, and she can stay. He completely ruins her alibi to leave. On his way out, something comes over him, and he just smiles while carrying little Emily.

Sara turns to face the pastor but then reaches for her phone so she won't have to listen but will only appear to listen. As her hand searches for her device, she realizes that it's in the diaper bag. Sorrowfully, she mildly stomps her foot in disgust. Her mother looks over at her and motions for her to pay attention. For a split second, Sara is caught feeling like a five-year-old again. She obeys her mom and focuses up front.

The service is compelling; the message is moving. It's focused on letting go of the past and knowing that Jesus loves you regardless of what you think. The words cut deep for Sara, and she grows uncomfortable. She begins to look around for Peter and the baby but is continuously bombarded by hushes from her mother and her pointing to look ahead. She doesn't want to let go of her past. She convinces herself that it may cause her to lose or forget about Emily. How can a god be so great and let her friend die? These are the sick tricks the fallen have implanted into her mind over the years. Even while their presence is still subject to wait at the dumpster, their work is at hand. She lowers her head and shakes the notion that she can be forgiven.

Eventually, the pastor wraps up the service and begins an altar call. While doing so, he instructs any and all that have been holding onto something, to come lay it at the altar. To give it to God and to let the healing process start. Sara doesn't move forward, but she does stand like the rest of the congregation. She blends in and lowers her head and acts like she is praying. She wants the service to end and to go home.

As her head is bowed, she feels a pressure rub along her back. She opens her eyes and sees a pair of pink sparkly heels with a pink and gold bow on top of them. She follows the shoes and stockings up and sees a dress that matches color and style of the shoes. She makes her way to the head and sees a peaceful old woman just smiling at her. It's one of the women that her husband absolutely adores. The woman continues to rub her back for a few seconds before she speaks.

"Come on, come with me," she takes her hands as if to lead her up front.

"No, thank you, ma'am, I'm fine right here," Sara resists and takes her hand and puts it at her side.

"I know you say you're fine. That's what brought you here today, you thinking your fine. I don't believe you're fine, child, and I think you know what I'm talking about. I know you don't really want to be fine. I know you want to be free."

Sara begins to tear up at the words of freedom, *How can this lady know what I'm feeling? How is this happening right now?* Sara lowers her head as she tries to hide from the truth that is being spoken to her at this very moment. Freedom has never been an option for her as she threw away the keys to her prison long ago.

"Listen, it's going to be okay. In fact, it's going to be better than okay. Now if you don't take my hand, then I'm gonna start screaming for no reason, and no one will stop me or help you because I'm old. So come on now. Let's go."

Chapter 17

"Come on and walk with Me, Sariel. I have a new protection job for you." The Master then turns to walk away from Ramiel and Sariel.

"Yes, sir. I'll talk to you later, Ramiel." Sariel then turns, catches up, and walks side by side with the Master, leaving Ramiel behind.

A few moments pass before either says or does anything besides walk. The Master turns His head toward Sariel and then waves His arm in the air. While He does this, Sariel turns his attention toward the Master and doesn't witness the effect that His wave has caused. Immediately as He puts His arm down, they walk through a portal and are transported to the front foyer of a church. Gold is replaced with tile, and all of heaven's majesty is replaced with wood, paint, and information pamphlets. No one is in the foyer as the service has already started and is, in fact, starting to wrap up.

"Listen to Me, Sariel. Things are about to change for you. This is going to be hard. This will be harder than anything you have ever faced," the Master tells him as they walk toward the sanctuary entrance. "They will know that she is a follower, and they will come at her and her family like never before. It's different for protectors when they are responsible for someone who follows. The enemy will lay on a full assault and siege over her. I need you to fight harder than ever before."

"Yes, sir, I will. I won't let You down like I did with Sara. I can't thank You enough for the opportunity to redeem myself. I'm so sorry that she didn't choose You. I will do everything I can to help this individual and to love them like I did her," Sariel states, not paying attention to his surroundings as he talks with the Master.

They both make it to the entrance and phase through the doors and into the sanctuary. Sariel is immediately met with familiarity as he recognizes his surroundings. He knows these pews, these walls, some that are in attendance, and he definitely remembers the big five, who have, in fact, grown even more since he last saw them. He sees the pastor of the church praying over some people at the altar, and then he sees her—Sara. Wrapped in death and mud, her soul is disgusting as it leaves a spiritual stain with each footprint left behind as she moves. Her hand is covered in love and light as Sariel also notices an elderly woman guiding her to the front.

The older woman's protector consumes the building at thirty-seven feet tall. He's not slow, he's not statuesque, he is a behemoth of power and love. The elderly lady guides Sara to the altar, but they don't go to the pastor. The additional four of the big five are waiting for her, as the group of ladies wraps themselves around her in absolute love and majesty. Sariel is able to see the Master as He is shown in each and every one of their souls as they make a cocoon of safety and power around her.

The big five, in addition, move in place and follow their ladies as they also squeeze in as much as possible to create a safe haven around the now six ladies. Their wings and bodies are too much for the altar area as half of three of the protectors hang outside of the building, causing the fallen that were waiting at the dumpster to be pushed even farther away. Sara, covered in filth and darkness, is now entirely surrounded by righteousness. Overwhelmed and humbled by what he sees, Sariel drops to his knees and begins to cry tears of joy.

"Sariel, it's not going to be easy. She's going to struggle and fight her past as she looks on her daughter. She's going to be reminded of false guilt from time to time as she takes her time letting go of a lie the enemy told her. But in all this, she will be okay. I will be with her, and so will you."

"Master, I am not worthy. I am not worthy. This is too much. I can't thank you enough for this. I don't know what to say."

"I love you, son, but I did this for her a long time ago. I have always provided this for her, and you know that. You really need to be thanking her. She chose Me. She is choosing to follow, and there is nothing greater, or that can bring Me more joy than what is happening right now with her."

"Thank You. You are holy. Holy, holy are You, Lord God Almighty," Sariel praises his Master as he witnesses her choice come to fruition, and Sara begins to take hold of it.

The Master helps Sariel off the floor, and they make their way down to the altar. As they walk, each stride grows ever so slightly for Sariel. He notices growth in his legs. He looks down and witnesses his arms extend as he also sees his chest fill even more. By the time they reach the big five, Sariel is standing a massive eleven feet tall. His armor is brand new and divine as it's permanently activated over his body. The additional weight and size do not slow him down. He is merely, bigger, faster, and stronger than he has ever been before. As he makes his way as close as possible, he leans in to hear what is taking place with Sara. Suddenly, the spiritual world is invaded with noise and light.

Over five thousand angels appear and line the skies as they are assembled across the heavens. Light radiates through the church and galaxies as their presence is righteous. As their fallen brothers once exhibited a wave of death, so these angels display a wave of forgiveness and life. Shouts of joy, gratefulness, love, peace, wisdom, and mercy are cast down on those with Sara. The angels are so loud with their praise that it's almost deafening. The pressure of their words coming with such force cause the eardrums of those listening to cancel out any other noise, thought or distraction. Sariel quickly adapts to the sound and listens to their words.

"You are worthy, our Lord and God, to receive glory and honor and power, for You created all things, and by your will they were created and have their being." And others shout, "The Lord is my strength and my song, and He has become my salvation. This is my God, and I will praise Him."

Praise and worship come from their lips, and as powerful as the angel's display is, their words are soft and pure, full of peace and life. The heavenly party that Ramiel had told him about is beginning to take place. Sariel bends over and tries to squeeze in between the massive protectors to hear what the ladies are saying to Sara. Between the noise and his large brethren, Sariel is only able to catch a few words every so often.

"Child, it's going to be okay." Followed by, "We know what happened. We were here. We remember."

Sariel pushes to try and hear more. "Sara, it's not your fault. He loves you so much, and He forgave you even before you put that seatbelt on."

"Sariel, come here. Look at this." The Master puts His hand on his shoulder to bring him back to an upright position while His other hand points toward home.

He stands erect and follows the Master's finger. They both watch as a beam of light comes crashing down on top of Sara. It completely consumes her body as the light acts as a running faucet, releasing cleansing water over her filthy soul.

"What is happening? Is everything alright?" Sariel is in awe as he witnesses the event. It takes him a moment to realize what is going on. He's never seen this happen before like this. Back when he was a recorder, it was different from his position and perspective, but he had never witnessed it first hand or this close.

"Yes, everything is fine. In fact, it's actually the beginning of becoming great. That beam is a representation of Me and my power of repentance. It cleans off as much as possible until they are reborn, new from sin and death."

Sariel watches as dirt and filth fall by the wayside of Sara's body. The heavenly host erupts with praise as the beam connects with Sara. They manage to exceed the noise that they expelled earlier by three fold. More passionately and with more intensity, the choir is putting on a show like no other. Sariel is overwhelmed with excitement and begins to join the festivities himself. He jumps, sings, dances, and shouts. All while the five little ladies speak into Sara's life.

A few minutes pass, and the party hasn't stopped or slowed down in the slightest. The difference with whats happening now is that one of the ladies has removed herself from the group and has made her way over to the pastor. A few short moments pass, and then she returns only to lead Sara toward a small room located by the baptismal tank.

"You're gonna love this next part. Watch this," the Master grins from ear to ear as He speaks to Sariel.

"Well everyone, Sara has decided to get baptized today. Come on, isn't He good?" the pastor raises one hand in the air and leans back in place as if the words he spoke pushed him back. He regains his posture and heads toward his office to change for the event.

Sariel watched the pastor intently as he made his announcement, excited that his little princess was going to become a follower. He watched as the beam of light followed Sara in that small room where she was changing clothes. She was still dirty, but not to the extent that she was when she entered the service today.

Moments pass and the door handle turns as it's pushed open to present Sara in shorts and a T-shirt. From the physical world, one could see that she had been crying, but that her face is showing relief and happiness. Peace falls over her as she is calm and ready.

The elderly woman takes her hand and leads her to the baptismal area that is behind the center section of the stage. She takes a few steps and reaches the stairs of the tank. Sara turns and hugs her friend that has helped her during this morning's service. She then turns and follows the steps as they rise and fall into the water-filled birth canal. Before she makes it to the top, the Master and Sariel make their way over to the tank standing at its first step.

As her first toe hit the water on her descent into the tank, an additional twenty-five thousand angels appear. Spiritually, the sound is incomparable. The battle cry of praise and victory roars through the air, causing any fallen within a twenty-mile radius to know what is happening here today. In fact, the pressure of the praise is so intense that it creates a storm of holiness to wipe away any and all fallen in the vicinity. Even the fallen that had been pushed back and beyond the dumpsters are now being slung by the strong winds to vacate the area entirely. The power that is produced is utterly cleansing.

Each step down and further into the water, the roar grows louder. All spiritual beings in attendance are in a state of euphoria with what's taking place. Sariel can't help himself but weep even more tears of joy. He remembers all the battles, all the prayers, all the mess and junk that the world offered and put in front of her with his overall small time watching and protecting her. Everything that happened and it still isn't ever enough to push the love of the Master away. Even when she rejected Him, He always loved her and had prepared and sacrificed for her for moments like this, and the eternity they will soon spend together.

At this time, Sara has fully entered the tank, and now the water is just above her waist. Sariel is able to see that as her body passed through the water, the parts of her body that were submerged had begun to thoroughly cleanse themselves. As if the filth were oil, it could no longer stick to her body. He begins to grow with excitement and anticipation as he witnesses the cleansing. His body language and emotion would be best described as a child waking up on Christmas day to a room full of wrapped presents.

The pastor begins to speak with Sara and tells her what's going to happen. He comforts her as he tells her how excellent and beautiful it is to be born again and the new sense of life she will have after rising from the water.

As the pastor continues to speak, the Master makes His way into the tank to join them. As He takes His place in front of Sara, He then lowers His hands into the water. The filth and death that separated from her submerged body quickly finds its way into His hands, as if they were a vacuum sucking up all that wasn't holy.

The pastor completes his instructions to Sara, and she grabs her nose with one hand, and the other grabs her wrist that is now over her mouth. Time begins to slow down as he utters the name Jesus Christ and lowers her body into the water. The angelic host in attendance, now over thirty thousand, erupt in silent praise as Sariel is fixated and only concentrating on the Master and Sara. He blocks out any noise other than the water, Sara, and his Master. He watches as she is fully submerged and death and sin are separated from her body. As it floats on top of the water and before she is raised up and back into its filth, the Master collects it all. She then proceeds to rise from the clean water and is embraced by her Master. As they connect, all of the tarnish of sin and death explode from His hands and shoots across creation as far as the east is from the west. The beam that was shining down on her is now gone as she is held by the Master. In

115

a twinkling of an eye, He disappears from all sight and Sara's soul shines. Like that of a nuclear bomb, the ferocity of light that sweeps through the atmosphere is powerful beyond measure. She is a new creature, pure and white as snow.

Everyone in attendance, spirit and flesh, erupt with shouts and clapping of the hands as she comes out of the water. Three additional angels suddenly appear beside Sariel, one each for her east, west, and south as he is responsible for her north. Sariel takes a spin to meet his new comrades, and as he turns completely around to see who is watching his six, he sees a familiar face. Ramiel, his friend and brother, is the warrior angel covering his back. He quickly grabs his friend and embraces him. They both begin to laugh and shout at the happy reunion. Ramiel quickly turns Sariel's attention back to Sara as she starts to take her first steps out of the tank. Sariel jumps on top of the stairs and bends over, as if to take Sara's hand and assist her out of the water. He bends over and quietly whispers to her. As he lowers his head and she hears the words, his face is shown to her for the slightest moment possible. The face she saw when she was only a child and the face she saw the other night as she reminisced about the tragic accident. The face that was there when she thought she was alone.

"It's good to see you again. I missed you, my love."

About the Author

Creativity has always been more than a hobby for Robert Newman. With his colorful and vivid imagination, storytelling has been second nature since childhood. Over time speculative fiction and the "what if" question have become more of his focus as he guides his creativity toward writing and filling those holes. A devoted father to two little girls and a crazy in love husband to his college sweetheart, Robert enjoys spending time with his family, church activities, playing board games, going to the movies and traveling.

CPSIA information can be obtained
at www.ICGtesting.com
Printed in the USA
LVHW031006200519
618456LV00002B/291/P